I Thee Dead

Book 1 in the Wedded Bliss Mystery Series

Christine Lawrence

First paperback edition August 2024

Book cover design by Julia Stahl, Jules Creative Solutions

Editing by Ann Bynum

ISBN: 979-8-9910885-0-3 (paperback)

979-8-9910885-1-0 (ebook)

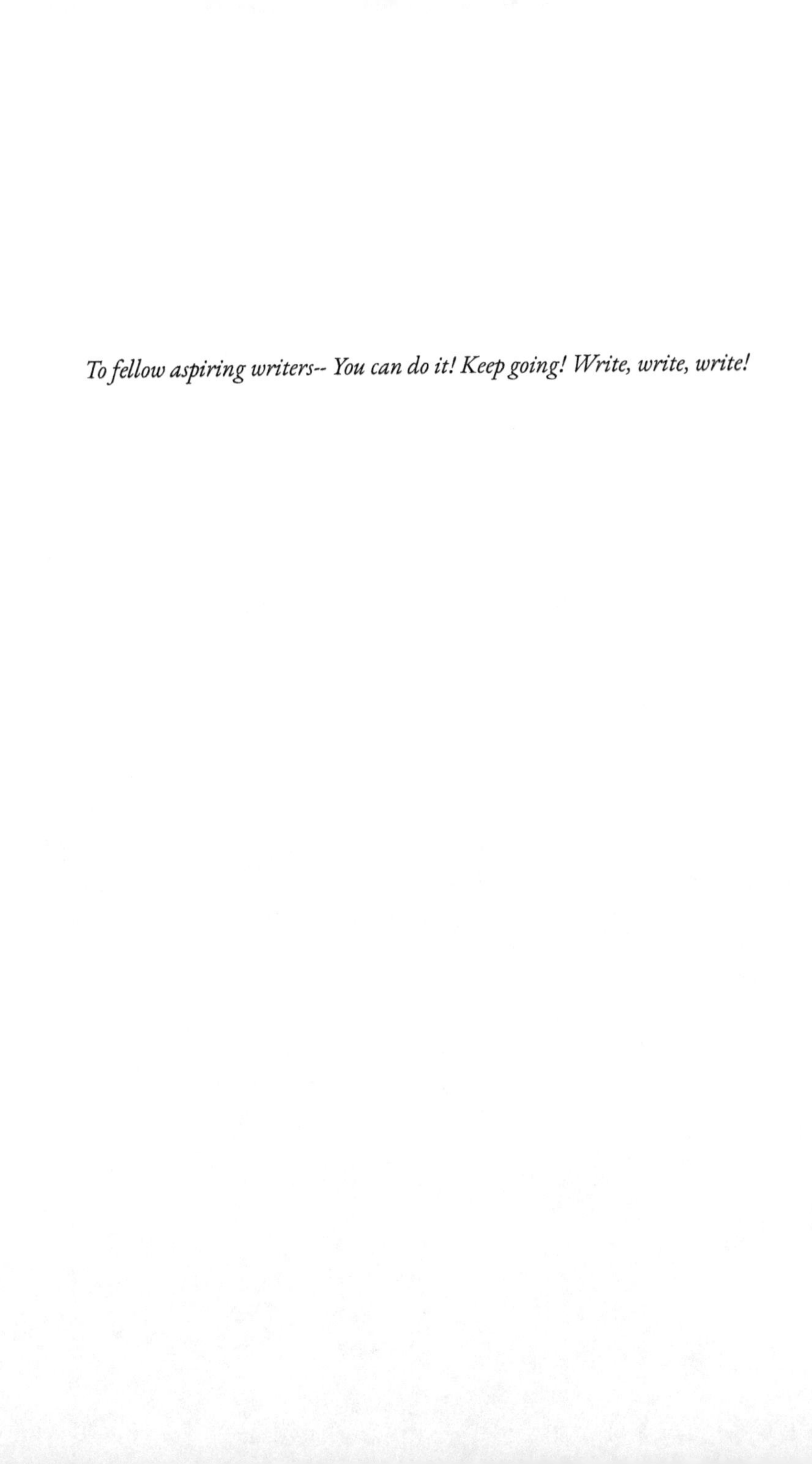

To fellow aspiring writers-- You can do it! Keep going! Write, write, write!

To fellow aspiring writers-- You can do it! Keep going! Write, write, write!

CHAPTER ONE

"Butterflies...butterflies? That's so pedestrian! I don't think so. I'll be the laughingstock of the country club!" Janie Coleman's golden curls quivered as she crossed her arms and stomped her tiny Louboutin covered feet, just like a child having a tantrum. Except this "child" was twenty-three and really a devil in a designer dress.

"Now, Janie, I am sure we could find something that would be more unique," I soothed, hoping to appease her.

This was not my first rodeo dealing with a difficult client, but she took the cake. A rich daddy's girl, who's never had to work a day in her life, had unlimited credit cards, new cars and anything she could ever want at her disposal, was now trying to plan her wedding, which is where I came in.

"Daddy says I have no budget, so money is no object. It has to be spectacular," she demanded.

"Let me check with my vendors, and we'll see what they can offer as an alternative," I suggested, hoping to prevent any future meltdowns.

Lord knows in the past few months there were more than enough.

"Totally, ooh! What if I had a large flower backdrop wall like Victor and Serena? Their wedding was so what I envisioned!" she bubbled.

Janie's "vision" of her special day had run the gauntlet anywhere from being held at an aquarium to a rooftop ceremony in Columbus, our state's capital. Victor, and his wife Serena Marquardt, were currently two of the country's most popular movie stars. Recently, they had wed in a lavish Greek villa overlooking the island of Santorini.

Okay, now she lost me. This was a new one. "You want to get married in Greece?"

"No, silly goose. I want all the glitz, the beauty, the media coverage." Janie's wide, baby-blue eyes glazed over. "Did you see Serena's dress? It was a Sophie Lily original! Hmmm, I wonder if I could ask them to make mine. I'll have to check."

As she pondered the complexities of that, I rolled my eyes. The celebrity wedding she spoke of cost over a million dollars.

"Let's narrow this down. We still need to finalize your theme. Have you given anymore thought about it since we last talked?" I mentally crossed my fingers and hoped she'd made a decision.

"I think I have," she replied.

Oh, thank goodness! "What did you decide?" Afraid of some horribly ridiculous response, I bit my tongue and inwardly winced.

"Diamonds are a girl's best friend!" Janie gushed.

"Oh!" Not at all what I was expecting. I almost burst out laughing but stopped myself in time. "Okay...diamonds. How do you think we should incorporate that?"

"Lots of glitz, glitter and crystals. Even my girls could wear glitter dresses. Plus, my shoes could be covered in Swarovski crystals. Oh. My. God. They are going to be so jealous!"

"All right got it. The colors will be silver and white?" I asked.

"And pink, my favorite color of course!" she blurted.

Of course, it was, I clenched my jaw to keep from sighing out loud and mentally rolled my eyes. A bit of guilt seeped into my frazzled brain, as I scolded myself for being such a negative Nancy.

Janie Coleman was short and petite. Her gorgeous ivory skin, blonde hair, and cornflower blue eyes had guys tripping over themselves trying to impress her.

I, Leah Jordan, was average. I was curvy and stood 5'7", with medium-length brown hair that had seen better days. My nose was slightly crooked from an old childhood injury, and the only things I had going for me were my gold-flecked hazel eyes and a nice pair of lips. Guys saw me as a friend, but never more.

Janie dressed in the newest designer clothes, and I shopped off the discount and knockoff racks. I worked for one of the most successful wedding planning businesses in Central Ohio, yet I was perpetually single. Those who can't do, teach, right?

The Wedded Bliss tried to provide each bride with a wonderful and memorable experience for the most important day of her life. Opened in 1982 by my mother Susan and my Aunt Sissy, it quickly became the most popular wedding venue in Ashford, Ohio. We had brides from all over the Central Ohio area clamoring to book an appointment.

We offered full-service wedding planning and vendors as well as the ceremony and reception site. When it first opened, the business was small and simple. There was one reception area, a small chapel and catering. As the years passed and the business grew, more was built on, which allowed the company to be able to provide more services and a fuller experience. Now it was my duty to carry on what my family began.

When I was eight, my parents were killed in a terrible car accident with a semi-truck on icy roads in January, and soon after, Aunt Sissy became my guardian. I learned the ins and outs of The Wedded Bliss like the back of my hand.

The main thing my aunt taught me was to listen to the bride, and even if they were frustrating and had crazy ideas, to have compassion and remember that this was the first day of the rest of their lives. Everyone wants it to be perfect, and we are their fairy godmother who can turn pumpkins into crystal carriages.

"Now we have your theme and the colors chosen, have you narrowed down the list of reception sites so we can do a final walk-through and book them?"

"Yes, I have. The governor's mansion and the statehouse," she stated.

"You are absolutely sure?" I asked.

Janie nodded. "Yes."

"All right, I will call up those locations, let them know they made the final cut, and confirm Saturday's appointments. I am calling in big favors for these to be held open for us until you make a decision, so please be sure you choose the one you really want for your wedding," I told her.

"Well, of course, silly. Morgan told me to pick whatever I wanted. He's the sweetest fiancé ever," she sighed.

Morgan Vanderbilt had no idea what he was getting into. He was a handsome man, who hailed from a lovely family and had a great job. Every family's dream son-in-law.

"I think we have everything for now. I'll set up and confirm the appointments for Saturday and prepare a list of alternative options you would rather have instead of the butterflies. You will need to meet with our florist now that we have your theme and colors as well as our decoration team. Sally up front can help schedule those for you," I explained.

"Sounds great. Morgan and I will see you Saturday," Janie agreed, picking up her purse.

I stood up, also, and walked her out.

I couldn't believe how much we arranged, considering at our first meeting, she only knew she wanted a wedding, a glamourous one, and she was going to wear white.

Once I returned to my office, I straightened up her client file. I also made a list of calls I needed to follow up on the next day. As I worked, my mind wandered to one of my business partners. I could tell something was bothering her a great deal, and I intended to find out what it was.

Chelsea Baker was a godsend. She managed the books, and the budget and made sure the utilities were paid. I didn't know what I'd have done without her. She was everything I wasn't, which was why the two of us were such an awesome team.

The woman looked exhausted. Her normally neat red hair was frizzy and thrown back in a messy ponytail. Even her clothes were wrinkly. This was not the well put together girl I was used to. Her amazing fashion sense always enabled her to choose clothing that complimented her slender 5'9" frame and porcelain skin. It was so nice to have her here. When Aunt Sissy left me The Wedded Bliss, I asked Chelsea to join the team and help with the books to lessen my overwhelming stress.

Friends since forever, she was the one person who knew all my secrets, had my back, and wasn't afraid to give me a kick in the butt when I needed it. For the past few years, our relationship had been strained. When I was eighteen, I moved out of Aunt Sissy's in Ashford to go to college in Columbus, but I remained in Ohio. Chelsea, however, relocated across the country to San Diego. We'd tried to stay in touch but failed miserably at times. Coincidentally, a few weeks after I moved back home to help Aunt Sissy with the business, Chelsea returned as well.

My childhood wasn't the easiest. Most people didn't know how to act around an orphan and treated me like a fragile piece of glass. It wasn't until I met Chelsea and Meg in third grade that I really began to flourish. Aunt Sissy was so thrilled I had friends she didn't care how often they came over.

Twenty minutes later, Chelsea popped her head into my office. "Hey, Leah. Got a minute?"

"Of course, what's up?" I finished clearing my desk and motioned for her to sit down.

She plopped down in a chair as she flipped open the notebook, she brought in with her. "Well, do you want the good news or the bad news?"

My stomach started to knot up. This had to be what made her appear so frazzled today. "Um, go ahead with the bad news."

"All right." She breathed out a heavy sigh. "I have been going over the books, and things aren't looking so hot. We are down about twenty percent from this time last year with what we're bringing in. If we don't figure out how to boost profits soon, we may need to revisit our business plan."

"That much? Holy moly! Why wouldn't Aunt Sissy tell me she was in this much trouble or ask me for help?" I wailed.

"Don't freak out yet. You know your aunt. She was feisty, but also loyal and stubborn. She probably just didn't want to tell you and worry you?"

I frowned and contemplated how to handle this new blow. "Maybe. I need to look over everything myself. Thank you so much for reviewing things, I really appreciate it."

Chelsea closed her notebook like she was putting the lid back on a poisonous snake cage. "No problem. I actually have some ideas. I'll bring them to our next office meeting. Which brings me to the last thing. I received an interesting voicemail from Morgan Vanderbilt."

"The groom? What did he have to say?" I asked.

"He was frustrated because he feels the bill we sent for the engagement party was outrageous," she muttered.

"Are you kidding me? They invited five hundred people, had six different food stations set up and a full-service bar!" I exclaimed.

"I know, and we had to pull it all together on short notice. I personally felt it was a wonderful event. I think he's just blowing off some steam. Lord knows I'd be stressed if I was marrying Janie Coleman," Chelsea chuckled.

"I am sure it will all work out. Don't let him get to you. I will look over the bill again too just to verify we didn't bill anything incorrectly." I scribbled a reminder to myself on a sticky note.

She closed her eyes for a second and took a meditative breath. "You're right. I will try to worry less about it when I have some other things to work on. Do you want to hear the good news?"

My shoulders slumped. "Yes, please. A little good news would be a breath of fresh air right now."

"Do you remember the Buckeye Brides' Wedding Guide?"

Buckeye Brides' Wedding Guide was a regional wedding guide company who put on several bridal shows in the area. Their booklets were found in local grocery stores, the library foyer and at wedding vendors' shops.

I nodded. "What about them?"

Chelsea held up crossed fingers and could hardly contain her excitement as she reported, "I may be able to get us the cover for their autumn issue!"

My eyebrows shot skyward. "No way!" I gasped. "How did you manage that?"

"Let's just say that I called in a favor," she answered with a wink.

"Oh, man. What's the catch?" I waited for the other shoe to drop.

"No catch. We only have to host the fall bridal show here in Ashford."

"Chelsea, don't you think it's a little soon? Why not hold off on that until we figure things out here first? It is a great opportunity, though."

"We can't wait too long," she cautioned. "You know it will be good exposure. Plus, think of all the people we could reach!"

"All right, all right. We'll discuss it more later. Right now, I need to run some errands. We'll catch up tomorrow?"

She rose, "Sounds great. I'm going to finish up and head out. See you in the morning!" she chirped on her way out.

I finished packing up my bag to go home. In an attempt to be optimistic, I told myself tomorrow would be a new day. Grabbing my jacket, I stopped at the doorway and shut off the lights. As I walked to our front hall, I paused at Aunt Sissy's portrait hanging on the wall.

Although she wasn't here anymore, I knew she was always watching over us. Vibrant, full of life and one heck of a businesswoman, I could only hope to be half the person she had been. Whenever the going got tough or I just missed her too much, I would stand in front of it and talk to her. She always listened.

This time was no different. "Oh, Aunt Sissy, I miss you to pieces. I'm trying to do the best I can to keep The Wedded Bliss legacy alive. Things may be a little rough at the moment, but I will do everything in my power to turn them around." I blew her a kiss and told her I loved her before shutting off the lights in the lobby and heading out the door.

It was still bright and sunny outside. Not too hot, a perfect summer day. I slung my bag into the passenger seat of my green Jeep Cherokee and climbed in. Ten minutes later, I pulled into my driveway.

I lived in a small but comfy tan house with burgundy trim. Only 1,100 square feet, it fit me just fine. Aunt Sissy left me a small trust fund when she passed, so I decided to invest some of it in my first home. The moment I stepped in the front door, two very plump and vocal felines pounced on me and gave me heck because they hadn't been fed yet and were obviously wasting away.

Patches and Oreo were a pair of stray sister kittens I'd rescued. They were my babies. Patches was a tortoiseshell with splotches of tan, orange and white covering her body. Oreo looked like the cookie, black on either end with white around the middle. At only a year old, they were quite an adventurous duo.

"Why, hello, my little ladies! How was your day?" I cooed, reaching down to pet them both.

As I stood back up, Patches started rubbing my legs. Her sister must have gotten distracted by something. She pounced off toward the kitchen. I heard an odd thud followed by silence. This was never a good thing as she was definitely the more mischievous of the two. I headed off to find her and her better-behaved sibling followed along.

"Oreo! What are you doing?" I called.

I discovered her sprawled out in the far corner, eating kibbles that spilled out of the bag I had just bought the night before. Of course, the one time I didn't pour it all into the storage container right away, the miscreant found a way to help herself.

She glanced up, barely acknowledging my existence, and went back to chowing down. I grabbed the plastic storage container and moved it over to the mess. I transferred what was left in the bag into the bin and shut it. Then I scooped the kibbles that remained on the floor into their bowl.

"All right ladies, that's all you. You two have your dinner. I'm going to get out of these work clothes."

I left the girls to their meal and headed to my room. While my job required me to dress in business attire, I was really a super casual kind of girl. Opening my dresser, I grabbed a white T-shirt and lavender yoga pants, got changed and slid into my favorite pair of gray fuzzy slippers. I made sure to get the next day's outfit ready before returning to the kitchen. A frozen pepperoni pizza won the contest to be dinner for the evening. I stuck it in the oven and set the timer for fifteen minutes.

Twenty minutes later, I was on the sofa, snuggled up with a blanket and my full-bellied fur kids on the floor at my feet. Before I began to eat, I turned on one of my favorite true crime TV shows. It was my secret guilty pleasure.

This was the life I'd made for myself. I had my business, my cats and a warm and comforting little house. I was happy, but it felt like something was missing. I just wasn't sure what that was yet.

The next morning, I woke up still on the couch, with Oreo's butt in my face and Patches lying over the top of my head. Some weird infomercial was blaring on the television trying to sell the newest fad in exercise equipment. As I glanced at the clock, hoping for at least another hour's worth of sleep, I noticed it read half past eight.

Crap! I had to be at the office at nine to meet with clients!

The poor cats were inadvertently thrown off me as I jumped to my feet and bolted for the bathroom. I took the fastest shower in recorded history, dashed back to my room and threw on underclothes, a navy skirt, a white blouse, pantyhose and all-purpose black heels. I yanked my brown hair up into a bun, applied a little lip gloss, grabbed my bag and flew out the door.

On my way, I sailed through a drive-thru to pick up a pastry and apple juice so my stomach wouldn't sound like a rabid tiger at the meeting. I finally reached work with just a few minutes to spare. Whew!

My clients had not yet arrived, so I had time to open up my office, get organized, and light a couple of gardenia candles.

"Good morning, Leah. You, okay?" Sally called out from behind the front desk.

I'd apparently breezed right past without noticing her. "Oh, you scared me! I didn't see you sitting there. I'm good. Thanks for asking. Stayed up late and ended up sleeping through my alarm. Will you please let me know when my nine o'clock appointment arrives?"

"Of course," she replied.

Sally Sweeney had worked at The Wedded Bliss longer than anyone else. She started when the business expanded, and they needed an office manager. A motherly type, now approaching sixty-five, she kept everyone in line and made sure everybody was taken care of. She stood 5'6" with short gray hair and warm brown eyes topping her average build. No one could ever replace her, and I was overjoyed she chose to stay on when I took over.

I settled behind my desk and pulled out a fresh notepad and intake form. Now I felt ready for my clients. Allison West and her fiancé Connor Adams were a couple who had been referred to us by a previous bride. We had recently held their engagement party, and they were coming to finalize their wedding details. There was not a lot of time to get things together as they wanted to have a short engagement. My desk phone buzzed.

"Leah, your appointment has arrived," Sally said.

"Thanks. I'll be right up," I replied.

I walked up to the front hall, exchanged greetings and led my clients back to my office. I motioned for them to take the chairs across from me.

I spoke first when they'd settled. "Good morning to you both, and welcome back. Let's start by having you tell me what you two envision for your wedding day?"

"I think the best way to describe what we want would be country chic," Allison answered.

"A country vibe with some fancier elements?" I asked.

She nodded. "Exactly!"

"How many people were you planning on inviting?"

"Approximately one hundred and fifty as of right now. We both have a lot of family and friends we want to share our special day with," Connor responded with a smile while taking his future bride's hand.

I made some notes. "Sounds great. Have you decided if you want to have the wedding indoors or outdoors?"

"My thought was an outdoor ceremony and an indoor reception," Allison said.

"What about if we decorate the party area like the inside of a barn, and the ceremony space outside could have straw bales as the seating," I suggested.

"Perfect!" she beamed.

"What time of year were you thinking?"

"We talked about October or early to mid-November before the holidays begin," Connor replied.

"October may be the better choice. It should be warmer than November. Have you thought about a menu or types of foods you would prefer?" I scribbled more notes.

"We want comfort food, good old home-cooking type dishes. Also, we'd like to have a cocktail hour between the ceremony and the reception with some simple appetizers," Allison responded.

"I think that sounds great! Our chef Stefan should have no problem working with you to create a menu that will meet all your needs. I can now is work up a basic quote from what we have discussed and get that to you for review. Why don't we tour the reception and ceremony areas we have available, and you can decide which one will work best?" I proposed.

"Wonderful—" Allison began to say but broke off as stomping and raised voices approached from down the hall.

Before she could continue, Janie Coleman and Morgan Vanderbilt barged into the office.

I shot up out of my chair. "Excuse me? I'm meeting with a client. What is going on here? Can I help you?" I demanded.

"We need to talk to you, NOW!" Morgan ordered at high volume.

I stepped around my desk and ushered them into the hall. I was fuming! What were they thinking? What could be so important that they had to interrupt a consultation like that? I poked my head back into the office to excuse myself.

"Allison and Connor, I'm so sorry. I need to step out for a minute to address something. Why don't you look through some of our photo albums from previous events and see if there are any ideas you may want to incorporate into your special day. Again, I apologize for this interruption. I will be back as soon as possible." I stepped out into the hallway, closed the door and went to speak with Janie and Morgan again.

My voice was curt. "Let's take our discussion to another office, and you can tell me why you are here." I motioned for them to follow me to an empty meeting room. We all took a seat at the table and Morgan spoke first.

"First of all, I'd like to speak to Chelsea again. I still feel we are not being charged fairly on the bill for the engagement party." Morgan began.

"If you would like to discuss your concerns further you may go to Chelsea's office," I said.

"I will," he grumbled and stormed out the door.

Tears rolled down Janie's cheeks as she looked at me with her eyes full of despair. "I'm so sorry, Leah, I'm unsure what's gotten into him. He usually doesn't act like this, but he has been under a lot of stress at work lately. He's been spending long nights at the office and taking these secret calls. If I try to answer his phone or use his computer, he snaps at me. I just don't know what to think!" she sobbed.

I grabbed a tissue from the desk, handed it to her and patted her shoulder. It sounded to me like Morgan was either into some shady business dealings or cheating on his bride, but it wasn't my place to delve into that. "Now, now, let's dry your eyes."

"Do you think there could be someone else?" she wondered, echoing my own thoughts.

I tried to ease her fears, though I believed them to be well-founded. "I've seen how Morgan looks at you. He is head over heels. Wedding planning is stressful, and it can bring out the worst, even in the best person. You mentioned a lot going on at his work. I'm sure he just has a great deal on his plate. You both do."

Janie sniffled and nodded. "Thank you. You're right. I'm probably over-reacting."

A few minutes later, a barrage of shouts erupted from Chelsea's office. Janie and I darted out of the room and down the hall to see what had happened.

CHAPTER TWO

"Don't you know who I am?" erupted the furious groom.

"I know exactly who you are, Mr. Vanderbilt, but that is no reason to act disrespectfully. I've gone over your bill numerous times and the contract you signed. I'm sorry, but everything was billed correctly," Chelsea explained.

"Hmph! You will be hearing from my attorney!" Morgan fumed and stormed past. "Let's go, Janie! Now!"

"Coming, sweetie!" his bride called as she turned to us with an apologetic look on her face. "I'll talk to Daddy and get this resolved. Please say you'll still do our wedding. I've wanted to be a Wedded Bliss bride for as long as I can remember." She hurried to catch up with her fiancé.

Chelsea met me at the door.

I touched her arm. "What the heck happened? It sounded like World War III."

Her face was flushed, and anger burned in her eyes. "That pompous jerk thinks because he can throw money around, that he should be awarded special privileges! One of these days, he is going to get his and learn that you can't live life acting as if you're above everything."

I patted her shoulder, trying to calm her down.

"Why don't you go for a walk and unwind? I need to see if I can save the appointment with Allison and Connor." I left Chelsea and returned to my office.

The couple were on their way out.

"I am so sorry! Please forgive anything you may have heard. There's been a misunderstanding, and it's being handled. I apologize. We'll continue if you'd like. I'll order some lunch, then we could finish discussing details while we eat," I suggested.

Connor tried in vain to force a polite smile. "That's very thoughtful of you, Ms. Jordan, but I think it is best if we go. We have a few more appointments to attend and a lot to discuss." The couple pushed past me and speed-walked down the hall in their obvious haste to escape.

Crap! We probably just lost a great bride because of the incident with stupid Morgan. I went ahead and made them a file in case, by the grace of God, they changed their minds.

I left the building and strolled down the block to a small café called Cozy Eats. After all this, I needed a break, and lunch sounded tasty. A local favorite, it served the best grilled cheese around. Thick pieces of Texas toast, gooey Cheddar and Asiago and a little onion made for one amazing creation. Add some potato soup, and I was happy as a lark.

A bite of my sandwich, a spoonful of soup, it was a good system. The longer I sat there, the more my mind dwelled on the current situation with The Wedded Bliss. I knew things weren't wonderful, but I guess hearing the words come out of Chelsea's mouth made it more real.

The present lack of weddings on the books and the fact that we had so many outstanding invoices from previous clients was discouraging. We needed to figure out how to get more money coming in and diversify our services. I hoped that the possible deal with the Buckeye Brides' Wedding Guide worked out. The one thing I had to do was put myself in a more positive mindset. WWASD? What would Aunt Sissy do? Whenever it felt like the cards were down, she just dug her feet in and kept on going.

A few hours after lunch, Meg, Chelsea, Sally and I gathered in the conference room. Scribbled in my notepad were a few ideas I came up with while I was eating. If we all put our heads together, I was sure we could come up with a lot more.

Meg Walton, our technology expert, rounded out our administrative staff. She, Chelsea, and I have been best friends since grade school, and it was so nice to have them both working with me. She was your average girl next door, standing at a short 5'4", with ash blonde hair, blue eyes and a smile that drew everyone in. She was expecting her first baby with her husband Joe, and the couple was over the moon with joy.

I started off the meeting. "Good afternoon. I want to go ahead and begin. We have a lot to talk about. The Wedded Bliss is a family, and right now we're in a tough spot and need to stick together. Due to some recent information, I have uncovered, we are at risk of foreclosure."

Sally gasped and placed her hands on her temples. "Oh no, Leah! That's terrible! I knew something was off, but I couldn't place my finger on it. Every single time I asked your aunt if everything was okay, she would assure me it was alright." She threw back her shoulders and clasped her hands in front of her. "We will get through this."

"I hope you're right. To start turning things around, let's brainstorm some ideas that could generate more income," I suggested.

Chelsea raised a hand. "I have several. First, I think we should expand our advertising. Next, we need to establish a social media presence. In today's world, just about everyone owns a smartphone and uses Facebook, Twitter, and Instagram. Creating accounts for the business would be free for the most part, and we can connect with more potential clients. Such pages would enable us to keep them updated on events, news, and any other pertinent updates."

"Hmm, that is a good idea." I jotted it down. "We've always relied on word of mouth and our reputation, but that's not enough with more competition these days."

"Another thing we can do is revamp our services list and create some new packages for the bride on a budget," she continued.

"That's a great one. It's not every day we get a client like Janie Coleman, who has an unlimited budget. A variety of packages and price points would allow us to cater to a broader customer base," I said.

Meg agreed. "In this economy, I think 'Bride on a Budget' packages could be very successful."

I raised my pen. "I've got one. What if we started offering anytime weddings?"

The other ladies remained silent and stared at me as if I had grown two heads.

"What are those?" Sally asked, breaking the awkward silence.

"There are couples that don't necessarily need all the bells and whistles of a big ceremony, but still want to get married in a nicer place than the courthouse. So it would be a by appointment kind of thing. They could come in and have a short civil service," I explained.

"We've never done anything like that before, but I guess it could work?" Sally remarked with a shrug.

"Classy though, right? We want to still provide the same level of quality as we always have," Meg said.

"Yes, exactly," I agreed. "We can decorate our Lovebirds Chapel with a basic setup. Then we could offer some add-ons to personalize their experience."

"What about some new flyers and pamphlets or ads? I am sure some of the local vendors we work with regularly wouldn't mind if we dropped some off," Meg recommended.

"Excellent!" I approved.

A thoughtful crease appeared across the center of Chelsea's forehead. "We can handle the paper items, but ads might be a little pricey right now."

"Any other ideas?" I prompted.

"I think I have one!" Sally exclaimed. "What if we hold a bridal show here? Nothing huge, but when you mentioned the local vendors, it could help us all with marketing and be a good resource for our local brides."

"How would we turn a profit, though?" I asked.

"When I used to do craft shows, each exhibitor was charged a small booth fee. If we budget just right, we could use some of that money to purchase a big ad, and the rest of it would go toward our other bills. Plus, if we set up the social media accounts like Chelsea suggested, that's free advertising, and we could reach a large number of people," she explained.

"These are all great suggestions. Why don't we concentrate on some of the smaller or quicker result ideas first, then we can focus on fleshing out details for a bridal show? If we take on too much right now with a few upcoming events in the books, I'm afraid we'll overwhelm ourselves," I replied.

"You make a good point, Leah," Meg concurred.

It seemed like a great place to stop, so I closed my notebook. "If no one has any other suggestions, I think we'll conclude this meeting. Let's meet back in a couple of days."

We returned to our respective work areas.

Chelsea did propose some useful plans. I wasn't completely tech savvy, but I thought establishing an online presence wouldn't be too hard. Her other idea intrigued me about creating packages for the bride on a budget. With the recent change in the economy causing financial issues, especially for average people, a toned down, pocket friendly offering would still enable those couples to celebrate their love. According to current trends, more were looking for quality over quantity, smaller guest lists and simple yet special events.

When my mom and aunt started The Wedded Bliss, one of their goals was to provide services to each and every bride and make them feel exceptional, no matter their price point. High-profile clients would keep the lights on, but it was more about the heart.

It took me an hour to get through some last-minute calls and emails. Then it was time to work on the packages. Our place had a small chapel, a few larger rooms and an outdoor garden, as well as a gazebo. The best choices for the budget-conscious would be to utilize the chapel, the outdoor garden and the gazebo. They had the least setup involved.

The most basic one could include the use of the space, an officiant, a cake, some hors d'oeuvres and punch. Each level up would add a little more. By the time I finished, I had four packages that I was excited to share with the others. We would still need to determine price points, but it was a great start.

My last task for the day was to locate some items for Janie and Morgan's wedding. I needed to hunt down a coach, an ice sculptor, and glitter and sparkly crystals. I already had someone in mind for one of those things. Scott Webb was the best sculptor in Ashford. Whether it was ice, food, or pumpkins, his work was fabulous. We used him in the past, but time was short and the pieces we needed weren't necessarily simple.

A fifteen-minute drive across town brought me to his company, Kewl Ice. Scott was the owner and the main designer. I prayed he would be able to meet our deadline. I parked in front of his business and went inside. At the front desk sat Angela, his assistant.

"Good afternoon, Leah, here to see the boss man?" she asked with a smile.

"Yes, if he's available," I replied.

"Sure, let me page him. Can I get you a bottled water or anything?" she offered.

"No, thanks, I'm fine." I chose a magazine out of the rack in the sitting area and took a seat. A few minutes later, Scott appeared.

"Hey Leah, what brings you in?" he asked as he approached.

The man was a big squishy teddy bear, husky and tall. He always had the friendliest face and a great smile for everyone he encountered.

"Could we go into your office? I have a few projects I want to discuss."

"Of course, and I will get my notepad so I can take some notes," he agreed.

I followed him down the hall into a spacious room with three cushy burgundy seats, a wide mahogany desk and some filing cabinets. He took a seat behind the desk in a high-backed leather chair while I sat across from him.

Mentally crossing my fingers, I got right to the point. "This may be a challenge. I have a wedding in a couple of weeks that I need three items for. Is there any way you could have them done by Saturday?"

He let out a deep breath. "Whoa. That is tight. Why don't you tell me about the designs, and we can go from there," he suggested.

"Ok let's see, two of them will be smaller pieces and the third is larger. First, the bride would want a pair of glass slippers. She would also like a huge heart with their names and the date engraved. Then we come to the biggest piece, a castle atop a platform luge that would be used to serve cocktails," I babbled, then winced, waiting for his reply.

"I don't think the first two will be an issue. The castle may be the clincher. I would probably need at least three people laboring on it to get it completed in time, and that extra labor is going to cost a pretty penny. What kind of budget are we working with?" Scott asked.

I grinned. "Here's the good news, unlimited. So...are you in?"

The big man smacked his fist on his desk, making me jump, and laughed. "Done!"

"You are a godsend, my friend! Thank you so much, I really appreciate it," I gushed, reaching across to shake his hand. "Send Chelsea the bill and let me know if you have any questions. I'm off to my next stop."

"Not a problem. It was good seeing you. Don't be a stranger!" he chuckled.

"Of course, it's the height of wedding season," I called over my shoulder as I left his office.

Ashford had one transportation company in town located ten minutes southeast of Scott's business. If anyone had a Cinderella type carriage or knew where to find one, it would be Taylor Transportation. Ed Taylor was a longtime friend of Aunt Sissy's, and they had known each other for ages.

Walking into the office was like a homecoming. When I was still too young to really help Aunt Sissy around The Wedded Bliss, she always made sure to take me with her on all of her various errands. Whether she realized it or not, I was paying attention, even then.

"Leah! Well, aren't you a sight for sore eyes!" Flo Ingerham had been the secretary there forever, and she was like a grandmother to me.

"Sore eyes, or just a sight?" I giggled.

"Oh, you!" She reached out with her right hand, pretending to swat me.

"Is Ed around?" I asked.

"Sure is. Probably two pots in by now. You know the drill."

Thanking her, I headed down the hall and stopped at the first door on my left.

I peeked inside. "Is anyone home?"

"Nope, I ran away," Ed chuckled, waving me in. "Come on in, Leah-bug." He was the only other person besides Aunt Sissy who called me that. Tall and slender with salt and pepper hair, always parted down the middle with his bangs brushed to the right, he was infamous for his sweater vests. Today he sported a navy cable knit one over a long-sleeved white dress shirt.

"How have you been?" I asked, sitting down across from him.

"Not too bad, my dear. Can't complain. What can I do for you?"

Hoping my luck would hold out, I answered, "I have a current client with a special request, and I need your expertise. My bride wants to rent a Cinderella carriage to take her to The Wedded Bliss for the ceremony, and after the reception it would drive the newly married couple to their hotel. Do you have one in your fleet?"

He thumbed through a Rolodex on his desk but didn't find what he wanted. "I don't believe we do, but I think a friend of mine up north may just have what you are looking for. Let me give him a call and check. Mind if I follow up with you later? I gotta remember where I put his business card."

"Sounds great. One of the wedding party members is flying in today. As always, duty calls!"

We both stood up, and I leaned over to give Ed a hug. We exchanged our goodbyes, and I headed to my car. Two of the major items were taken care of check...check!

Janie and Morgan decided to fly all their out-of-town guests in for the wedding. As luck would have it, John Glenn International Airport in Columbus was only twenty-five minutes away. Driving didn't bother me. It was one of my forms of stress relief. I had fun cranking the volume up on the radio and singing at the top of my lungs, even if it was mostly out of tune. While we rarely handled transportation, I was pulling out all the stops to keep our clients happy. After all, they were paying over one hundred thousand dollars! It was my first huge event, and I had a lot to prove.

Morgan gave me a brief description of the groomsmen I was picking up. He told me he'd be six feet tall with short brown hair, green eyes and a muscular build. I hoped I would be able to pick him out of the crowd. He informed Caleb Hamilton that I would meet him at baggage claim.

I maneuvered through the maze of the airport parking garage to the area for arrivals. I tried to park my car closest to the entrance to Caleb's airline. Someone in the front row was just leaving, so I snagged the spot and hurried through the double doors to the elevators. Selecting the floor for baggage claim, I rode down, then walked over to the bank of arrival screens.

The monitor said Flight 584 from Cleveland was on time. I'd arrived a little early, so I took a seat across from the conveyor belt and waited. Soon, I saw people start descending the escalators. Then came the fun part, watching them try to figure out which bag was theirs and grab it off the carousel.

It brought back fond memories of being a kid, trailing along with my dad during the weekends on his routes. He worked for a local delivery company that shipped cargo by air. He picked the shipments up at the airport to deliver them where they needed to go. Once he finished, we would head to the parking garage, park all the way at the top and observe planes taking off.

If there was a chance before we had to get home, we would buy hot chocolates from one of the coffee shops and people watch at the baggage claim. My dad would make a game of it, trying to guess which bag matched which person and then create stories about them. It wasn't a fancy or expensive hobby, but he worked a lot of hours and tried to spend quality time with me whenever he could.

Travelers continued to enter the area and gather around the carousel. A few minutes later, a series of beeps sounded, causing the belt to start bringing out luggage from their flight. As the passengers swarmed, it became hard to see individual faces. I stood and moved closer to scan the crowd.

Out of the corner of my left eye, I spied a guy wearing a ball cap, leather jacket, T-shirt, and jeans. He appeared to be around the right age and fit the description I was given. I headed towards him but had to squeeze through a group of people. Just as I reached him, a lady in front of me leaned forward to grab her bag. I came to an abrupt halt to avoid a collision, but ended up tripping on my own feet and flew straight into the arms of one of the most handsome men I'd ever seen.

"Why, hello to you. Are you okay?" he asked, looking down at me with a smile.

When our eyes met, it felt as if the breath was sucked out of me. Like, I stopped breathing for just a moment. I pulled myself away, stood upright, and brushed myself off.

My purse had fallen in the altercation and, much to my annoyance released its contents all over the floor. I scrambled to pick up every receipt, piece of gum, a tin of mints, lip balm and some loose change. Once I had it all gathered and shoved back where it came from, I rose and faced him again, ignoring the heat rising in my cheeks.

He cleared his throat. "Did you miss something?"

I glanced down but couldn't see anything else until I looked over at Caleb. On the end of his finger, to my absolute horror, swung a pair of my underwear. Oh my god, I totally forgot it was in my bag! I snatched them and stuffed them in my pants pocket.

"Funny, I didn't picture you as a bikini kind of girl." The gorgeous man crossed his arms in front of his chest and winked.

"It's not what you think," I mumbled, refusing to look him in the eye. Why couldn't the ground open up and swallow me? Or maybe I would spontaneously combust. My face sure felt hot enough.

Oreo, one of my cats, was not only a food thief, but also had an affinity for snagging unmentionables. A few weeks ago, on my way out of the house, I caught her playing with a pair of my underwear. Since I was in a hurry, I got them away from her, shoved them in my purse and forgot they were there. He wasn't wrong. I was a full brief kind of girl and only wore the skimpy ones on laundry day.

He smirked. "Then what is it?"

"It's not important," I muttered and stuck my right hand out. "I'm Leah Jordan. I presume you are Caleb Hamilton?"

He shook mine in return and grinned. "The one and only."

Oh my. His teeth were as perfect as the rest of him. My heart gave a little flutter.

"It's nice to meet you." Good grief! Couldn't I think of something more creative to say? I threw my bag on my shoulder and gestured for him to follow me toward the elevators. "Janie and Morgan sent me to pick you up. Ashford is a twenty-five-minute drive from here. Then you can get ready with the rest of the groomsmen and relax before the pre-wedding activities begin."

"Wait a moment, who are you?" Caleb asked, trying to keep up with me.

"I'm the wedding planner. I figured you knew they were sending someone to retrieve you," I replied.

"Yes, but I thought a driver would be here."

They were busy finishing the final details and forgot to arrange one. I hope I am an acceptable replacement." I explained, continuing toward the elevators.

As we reached them and waited for the doors to open, I found myself glancing at Caleb out of the corner of my eye. He had beautiful green eyes. One even had a little fleck of gold. He also smelled so good and was so masculine, with full, plump, kissable lips. The elevator opened, startling me out of my observations.

He stuck out an arm to keep the doors open. "After you."

Wow! Chivalry wasn't dead after all! I stepped in and Caleb followed. The next few minutes after I pushed the button were filled with an awkward silence.

Once we reached our parking level, I fled the claustrophobic box and made a beeline for my car. I unlocked it and popped the trunk so my passenger could stow his bags.

He nudged my arm. "If it makes you feel better, I'll drop my drawers so you can have a glimpse of my underwear. Then we'd be even."

I stifled a laugh and teased, "As much as I appreciate the offer, I'll pass. You can keep your holey tighty whities to yourself."

He grabbed at his chest. "Ouch! That's harsh." He raised an eyebrow. "Who said I wear tighty whities?"

I started to choke as the now familiar heat of embarrassment crept up my face. "Ahem, may we please change the subject?"

Caleb relented. "All right, tell me about Ashford."

"You've never been here before?"

"Nope."

"It's a sleepy little town, small but vibrant. Known for its charm. We only have two banks, a library, a courthouse, a grocery store, some churches, a couple factories, restaurants and retail shops. Most of the population consists of longtime residents and families. Ashford takes a lot of pride in its community." I felt like a tour guide or a narrator for a documentary on small town life.

"Reminds me of a Rockwell painting," he chuckled.

"Not exactly. Everyone knows your business and gossip travels faster than light. As a teen, I wanted nothing more than to go out, see the world and have adventures. It just wasn't in the cards. I went to college, got a job in a lab after graduation and never left Ohio," I sighed.

"How did you find yourself back in Ashford, if you don't mind me asking?"

I shrugged. "There were a few reasons. My Aunt Sissy became sick, and a relationship I was in came to an end. I also lost my position around the same time, so it ended up working out. When Sissy passed away, she handed down the family business to me. Now I am trying to continue the tradition, while forging my own path to establish a reputation for myself. Hers were some big shoes to fill."

Oh my gosh. Why was I telling a stranger all this personal information? I kept glancing at him from the corner of my eye as I spoke. He didn't roll his eyes or make faces. Caleb was genuinely listening and taking an interest in what I said. Maybe that's why. He made me feel comfortable, and it was easy to talk to him. It'd been a while since I felt that way about a guy.

"I'm very sorry to hear about your loss. My condolences. Do you regret it?" he wondered.

"Coming back to Ashford? No. To be honest, my mindset has changed. I'm older, and I appreciate it now, more than I did before. The city was great, don't misunderstand me, but there is just something about small town living. Do you like Cleveland?" I asked.

"I do. Downtown has a lot to do. Great restaurants, too. The rat race does get old. I will have to be certain to enjoy all that your community has to offer while I'm here," he commented.

It was refreshing how the conversation just flowed for the remainder of the drive. With my ex-fiancé, it was like pulling teeth at times, or he would shift the focus and make it all about him. I really thought I knew him. We'd been together for almost three years, but I guess we don't always know people like we think we do.

We arrived at the Ashford Hotel, and I pulled into the lot and gave my companion a smile. "Here you go. Just check in at the desk, get settled in your room, and don't forget that Morgan wants you to call him. I hope you enjoy your stay."

Caleb stepped out of my car and retrieved his bag from the trunk. Then he came back up to the passenger door, leaned down and stuck his head inside. "Thanks, I appreciate it."

He closed it, and as I watched him walk away, I sucked in my breath. Wow, he was so handsome and there was something really attractive about him. I couldn't recall feeling an instant connection like that with anyone before. However. the rational side of my brain kicked in. Aunt Sissy's lists of rules played loudly in my head. Rule number one: You must always be professional. The ingrained voice of my aunt skipped ahead to rule number four: Never get too friendly with the client or their guests.

Rats!

At the moment, my list of tasks for the day was completed, I looked forward to being home where I could unwind with my fur children and prepare myself for my last meeting with Janie and Morgan to review all the final details of the rehearsal dinner and wedding. They had also planned days of different activities for their guests between now and the ceremony we needed to confirm.

My stomach made a horrendous growl, reminding me that it was mealtime, and I was famished. I swung through a drive-thru and picked up a greasy cheeseburger, fries, and a big soda. Not usually my first choice, but it was quick, easy, and I felt like splurging. I drove to my house where I would eat, feed the kitties and head to bed. The coming days would be busy, and I would need to be on top of my game.

Chapter Three

I felt like I'd barely put my head on the pillow when my alarm clock blared its offensive tone at me to get my butt up. I smacked the snooze button. After the third time, a heavy weight landed on my chest. Hot breath wafted into my face. I pried open an eye and saw Oreo staring at me.

She meowed, nuzzled me with her head and began kneading my collarbones with her paws. I reached out to pet her and closed my eyes. A few minutes later, her purring grew quiet, and I felt her breathing on me again. Aww, my adorable kitty is going to cuddle with her mommy. Just as I finished that thought, a hard swat on my nose caused my eyes to fly open. The offender jumped off the bed and darted towards the kitchen.

"Ow! Okay, okay, you want breakfast, I get it," I grumbled, tossing off the covers and sliding into my slippers.

Stumbling down the hall, I rubbed my face as I followed her. I filled their food and water dishes and gave them a few morning pets before I shuffled back to my bedroom to get ready for the day.

A quick shower woke me up a little more. I dried my hair, slid in a cute rhinestone clip, and chose a pair of black slacks with a lilac blouse to wear. On my neck and wrists, I spritzed a little cologne, and I was all set. I swung through the kitchen, pulled a drink from the fridge and left for The Wedded Bliss.

Chelsea was already there when I arrived. Walking by her office door, I could hear her on the phone. My first task was to meet with Chef Stefan to make sure everything was on schedule for today's final wedding reception tasting. As I entered the kitchen, wonderful aromas filled my nostrils.

I started with a cheerful greeting. "Good morning!"

"Leah, how are you? Coming to check on things?" he asked with a return smile.

"You know me all too well. I'm checking off my to-do list. Do you have everything you need?" I inquired, reaching out to pilfer a piece of cheese off the counter.

"I think we're doing great. There shouldn't be a problem getting done with the couple by eleven-thirty," he answered.

"Great, they will be going to finalize details with the florist and our decoration team. If I hear anything different, I will let you know." I replied, snatching another morsel.

"Wonderful! Unless you require any further assistance, I'll return to preparing."

"Of course! I don't want to bother the master at work." Before I could snag more cheese, Chef Stefan shooed me away. I scooted out of his domain and made my way towards my office.

Once I sat down at my desk, I pulled out the seating chart, the room layout, and the schedule of events so I'd be ready for the meeting. The gold-framed wall clock read eight-thirty, which gave me a half hour to make some follow-up calls to a few vendors for other clients and order new brochures with our summer specials.

The time flew by, and before I knew it, Janie and Morgan had pulled up out front. I met them in the foyer to welcome them in.

Her entire ensemble from head to toe was almost all pink. She wore a silk long-sleeved blush-toned blazer with a white blouse and matching skirt. Pink pointy heels with little bows adorned her tiny feet, and she carried a clutch with pink and diamond crystals.

Her future groom chose to be much less flashy in a navy wool jacket paired with matching slacks, a black tie, and a white dress shirt.

"Isn't Saturday going to be so beautiful? Daddy says it's supposed to be sunny and warm. Which will be perfect, of course, for my perfect self on my perfect day!" Janie exclaimed.

I thought I might throw up.

"Yes, dear, let's wrap this up. I must meet with an important client at one," Morgan interjected.

I motioned them to follow me back to the Love Room. We had set up a rectangular table with two chairs on one side and another for me across from them. Once we were settled, I motioned to Chef Stefan, who was waiting at the kitchen door, that we were ready to begin.

A few minutes later, our server Mara brought out a selection of soups on a beautiful, ornate serving tray. The aroma rising from the steam wafted up and into my nostrils. She placed it in front of our happy couple with cloth napkins and spoons. The samples looked amazing. I was glad I didn't have to make the decisions.

Once all of the options were arranged before them, Chef Stefan stepped forward.

"Welcome Ms. Coleman, and Mr. Vanderbilt. We are starting off today with three different soups that are elegant, and delicious and will be a great start for your guests." He gestured to the first bowl. "We have here a French beef stew, it's hearty and filled with beef, vegetables, herbs, broth, and red wine."

Janie picked up her spoon and took a small sip. "Wow, that is very good. What do you think, honey?"

Morgan shrugged. "It's okay. Not sure if it's the right one."

Jeez. I thought the bride was hard to please, but when it came to food, it looked like the groom was the difficult one.

"Let's move on to the next option. Here we have cream of Brie, with shallots and mushrooms. It's smooth, creamy and pairs well with many different wines," the chef explained.

I looked back and forth between the couple to gauge their reactions. This one seemed to be a hit. Morgan even opted for a second spoonful. The last offering was Pumpkin. They were not blown away. Mara removed the tray and returned to the kitchen to retrieve the next course.

Once the new plates were lined up for presentation, Chef Stefan began to describe them. "Next, we have the appetizer options. As we've previously discussed, there will be a table with a variety of cheeses, crackers, vegetables and fruits. We will also have servers walking around with caviar-topped canapes, bacon-wrapped figs stuffed with goat cheese and baked brie bites with a cranberry compote."

Janie chose a fig from the tray and sliced it in half. She took a bite, and I held my breath. She let out a little moan, and her eyes rolled back. "These are delicious! Darling, you must try one."

Morgan was on his phone again, and after much prodding and nagging, he finally tried one. "Yeah, they're good."

Ugh. He could at least feign a little more excitement or interest.

At last, the main courses came out. Roasted lamb chops with garlic and herbs and chicken Francese. Each one was served with rosemary mashed potatoes, and grilled asparagus. Janie had selected the lamb chops because they were Morgan's favorite. He was more focused and excited about these options.

We left the room and let the couple discuss amongst themselves for a little while. Twenty minutes later, I returned to see if they had made their final choices, see if they had any questions and conclude the appointment.

My stomach was in knots anticipating their answers. I really hoped the bridezilla, or the groom of gloom didn't cause any last-minute issues as the deadline was very tight.

I took a seat back at the table. "All right, have we decided on the options Chef Stefan presented today?"

Janie nodded vigorously. "We have. It was difficult, but I think we're happy with our selections."

I let out a deep breath. Thank gosh!" Great! Let's start with the soup. Which one did you want to go with?"

"Cream of Brie," she responded.

I noted it. "And what did we think about the appetizers? Did you want to do all three of them?

"Hmm, I think we'll just do two. The figs and the caviar-topped canapes. Does that sound good, dear?" She looked over at her groom and elbowed him in the ribs.

"Ow!" He rubbed his side. "Yes, that sounds great, my love."

I continued writing. "Great. So that just leaves the entrees. Are we happy with both options? Did you want to make any changes?"

Janie glanced over at her fiancé, waited a brief moment then looked back at me. "Yes, those two choices will be perfect. Thank you."

"If there is nothing else, I will give the chef your final selections. I know you have other appointments to attend. Speaking of appointments, don't forget we are meeting again tomorrow morning to go over the final details for the rehearsal dinner," I reminded them.

"Thank you, Ms. Jordan, we'll see you tomorrow," the satisfied bride promised as she gathered her purse from the floor and stood up to leave.

Morgan gave a half wave and mumbled his goodbyes barely looking up from his phone. Mara returned and began clearing the rest of the table. I walked over to the kitchen and stuck my head in the door. Chef Stefan was chopping up vegetables while humming along to music on the radio.

"Hey, just wanted to give you the final selections for the Coleman and Vanderbilt wedding," I called out.

He looked up from the cutting board. "Great. Were they happy? It was hard to tell at times."

I nodded. "They were. You chose some very delicious dishes. I am so relieved it went smoothly." I grinned and ripped a page from my pad and handed it to him. "I wrote down everything. Let me know if you have any questions. I'm going back to my office. I'll see you later."

Chef Stefan smiled and took the paper. "Thanks, Leah."

After finishing up at the office yesterday, I was so mentally exhausted. The rest of the day was a blur. There wasn't a coffee cup big enough to get me through another meeting with Janie and Morgan again. It felt like a bad case of déjà vu. But here we were.

"Good morning. I'm glad you both could join us again. We have a lot to talk about, but I think we can cover it in a timely manner," I began.

The bride wore that perpetual gormless smile that only the most spoiled of children can conjure up. "Sounds fantastic."

"First, let's go over the rehearsal dinner." I consulted my notes. "Per the schedule we created, we have guests arriving at five-thirty, and the meal at six-thirty. Is that correct?"

"Yes, it is," she answered.

Morgan remained silent and looked less than thrilled to be there. He had his nose buried in his phone, typing away and mumbling to himself.

I raised an eyebrow at his blatant disinterest but continued. "Great. The soup Friday night will be tomato bisque and oysters Rockefeller for appetizers. For the main course, you have selected pan-seared salmon, beef medallions bordelaise with pan-roasted wild mushrooms, grilled asparagus and a mixed salad. Dessert will be chocolate mousse."

"Actually, I think we should have crème brûlée instead," Janie decided.

"That shouldn't be a problem. Are there any other changes that we need to make?" I asked.

"Not really, except the number of guests will be twenty-five now, not thirty, as originally planned," Morgan answered.

I scribbled a notation. "All right, I can let the staff know."

"There is one thing we want to modify for the wedding," she added.

One *more* thing, I corrected it in my head. "What adjustments would you like to make?" I gritted my teeth with each word. It took everything I had not to pull my hair out. Why, after all these weeks and all the time we've put into the event, would she have to change things now?

"I feel we should include a seafood station for our reception. Not any of that cheaper stuff. It needs to be fresh."

Little did she realize Ohio was not exactly the seafood capital of the Midwest.

"It would have to be flown in, and that would cost money. Are you sure that's what you want to do?" I asked pointedly.

She gave me an incredulous, wide-eyed stare. "Of course! Fish is Daddy's favorite."

Okay, seafood. Great. I crossed my fingers that Chef Stefan's connections could come through.

The rest of the wedding attendees were set to arrive over the next couple of days. Janie wanted to have his and her activities for her bridal party and some of their important guests. We scheduled a spa day for the ladies and a golf outing for Morgan and the guys the following day. I wanted to stop by each location and make sure everything was running smoothly, then I would head back to the office. The rest of the day Janie planned herself.

A lunch for the bridal party, and their bachelor and bachelorette activities would commence in the evening.

This event was so important not only to the couple, but to The Wedded Bliss and our future. I caught myself wringing my hands and legs bouncing more than usual in the past few weeks. Anxiety was running high and while I was confident in our staff that the event would go off without a hitch, there was still a tiny seed of doubt that I had what it took to live up to my legacy.

I first visited the Mario Icabano Salon and Day Spa. Close to Ashford, it was the premiere, albeit the only full-service salon and day spa in Barton. Ann, the owner, was an old friend from high school. We always tried to give each other business whenever possible. Janie had invited her five bridesmaids, her mother and future mother-in-law. Upon arriving, I stopped at the reception desk.

"Good morning, Leah!" She reached across and gave me a big hug. "Welcome to Mario Icabano Salon and Day Spa," she greeted me.

I smiled. "Hey, Ann! Has the Coleman party arrived?"

"Yes, let me check their current location." She clicked a few keys on her keyboard and checked the screen. "Looks like they are currently in the massage rooms. Did you want to go back?" she offered.

I shook my head. "No, that's fine. I just wanted to confirm they made it and got started with their experience.

"Of course. It's all perfect, and they are on track to finish by five. Is there anything else we can do for you, Leah?"

"Nope, Thanks, hun! I'll see you again soon," I answered with a wave.

Next, I headed to the beautiful Ables Golf Course, just outside of Ashford. This time of year, if wives couldn't find their husbands, they had to look no further. I followed the long drive to the clubhouse and parked. As I walked through the door, my eyes were assaulted with plaids, shirts, shoes and golf equipment. I approached the desk and read the guy's name tag.

"Good morning, Dean, I'm Leah Jordan, from The Wedded Bliss. I thought I'd check in to make sure the Vanderbilt party arrived and met their tee time," I said.

"I believe so. Let me verify." The young man checked his computer. "Yes ma'am, they are sitting in the lounge right now. Did you need to speak to them?"

"Actually, if you'll point me toward them, that would be great," I replied. After the big fuss with Morgan, I thought it would be best to stop by personally and foster some goodwill.

Dean directed me down the hall towards the lounge and to the left. Once I located it, I remembered lounge was kind of a loose term. It was really more of a good old 'boys' club. Several of the tables were occupied by golfers and many conversations involved their games, so-and-so's handicap and who had the best nine. The décor consisted of deep shades of hunter green, burgundy, navy and gold, while the walls were covered with pictures of the course, its members and various types of golf memorabilia. I spotted Morgan's group towards the back.

I threaded my way through the other tables to reach them and pasted on a cheerful smile. "Good morning, gentleman. I hope everybody is well. I wanted to come by and make sure you were having a lovely time."

"It's going great. We're waiting for a couple more people to arrive," Morgan replied.

"If there is anything you need, please notify us." I wished everyone a good game and fled before he could think of some reason to complain.

I returned to The Wedded Bliss, but before I could make it to my office, Chelsea approached me.

"How's your day so far?" she greeted me. I noticed her eyes sparkled with her usual liveliness, and she didn't look so worn out today.

"Hey, Chels. It's been going pretty well so far. You seem upbeat about something."

She grabbed me by the shoulders and started dancing around. "We got it. Leah, we got it!"

Confused, I bobbled along with her anyway. "Got what?"

"It! The fall cover of the wedding guide, it's ours!" she shrieked. "Can you believe it? This is going to be amazing! I couldn't wait to tell you. I just finished the conversation with them ten minutes ago!" Unable to contain her excitement, she did another happy dance.

I gasped. "That is awesome! What happens now?" This was just what we needed!

"They are planning to schedule the photo shoot, and Paula will reach out about organizing the bridal show."

"That's great! I'll write it down in my planner. Can you email me their contact information, so I have it? I need to finalize the Bride on a Budget packages and once everyone looks them over, I will get them over to the printer," I babbled. The anxiety over our financial situation must have been weighing upon me more heavily than I imagined.

"Of course, not a problem. Everything is really starting to turn around, I told you. Let me know if you have questions."

I think I must have floated to the break room where I grabbed a cold soda before reaching my office. Maybe Chelsea was right. Things would be just fine. After the fiasco with Allison and Connor, I hoped this opportunity and the new packages we were preparing to roll out would mean The Wedded Bliss would soon be booming with business. Finishing these packages was destined to be a challenge, but I planned to stay at my desk and work on them as long as I had to.

The next day, the Cupid Room looked astonishing. I had to give credit to our crew. They always did fabulous work! The color scheme for the rehearsal dinner was burgundy and silver. Tall arrangements of white roses with crystal accents adorned each table.

After guests began to arrive, I scurried to the kitchen to check in with Chef Stefan and the staff. Everyone bustled around, preparing and finalizing the dishes for the event. I found him over at the stove, speaking with the sous chef Tony.

"Sorry to bother you, Chef. I just wanted to touch base with you and see if you needed anything before the event got started?" I asked.

"Oh Leah, I think we've got it under control. Everything is coming together very well. We're on time, dare I say, running a little early, in fact," he replied.

"Great! I'll let them know they can begin. The salad will be out first, correct?"

"That's right, a spring mix with strawberries, walnuts, gorgonzola cheese crumbles with a poppy seed vinaigrette."

"Wonderful. If you need me, you can reach me on my walkie-talkie." I glanced down and began looking over everything left on my checklist. As I backed out of the kitchen doors, a server was on the other side attempting to come in, causing me to almost run into him. "Oh my gosh, I am so sorry! I should have been paying more attention."

"No problem, Ms. Jordan. My hands were empty. It happens to all of us," he replied with a smile.

He made his way into the kitchen, and I gathered my scattered nerves while I walked over to the Cupid room to check on the happy couple, who were greeting their guests.

"Good evening, you two. Janie, you look fantastic! Your outfit is beautiful," I gushed.

She wore a short, sparkly blue cocktail dress, with her hair put up in a tight chignon. Gold dangling earrings and silver heels completed her ensemble. Morgan was dressed in a stylish black suit with a handkerchief, which coordinated with the color of Janie's gown.

"Good evening, Leah. Thank you. The room is stunning," she said. Morgan just stood there, preoccupied until she nudged him in the side.

"Right, it looks nice. I see someone I need to talk to. If you'll both excuse me." He placed a chaste kiss on her temple and strode into the room.

I personally had misgivings about the whole thing and wondered if Janie simply wanted a huge wedding because it would make others notice and envy her. It would not be appropriate, however, for me to voice my opinion, so I pasted on a smile. "I hope you enjoy your party. If you need anything, let one of the staff members know and they can page me."

"Awesome. I'm going to find Morgan now. Later!" And with that, she was off.

Anytime we had an event, I stayed until after it was over. Just in case an issue arose, I would be close at hand to put out any potential fires. Plus, I had plenty of paperwork to keep me busy. The flyers for the new packages would be going out soon, and I wanted to compile a mailing list and send them out to our previous clients and the vendors we had worked with over the past few years.

First priority was the invitation Chelsea received from the Buckeye Brides Wedding Guide. I never signed anything without reading it word for word - another Aunt Sissy rule. My eyes scanned over the document. Everything seemed in order.

The fall bridal show would take place in October. They planned for over twenty vendors. The Wedded Bliss would get a portion of the admission tickets and a deposit for using the facility. We would be on the cover and the featured vendor in October, November and December and be charged half off an inside ad for The Wedded Bliss. I signed the contract and set it aside to give to Chelsea later so she could write a check and send it off.

Next, I had the latest wedding magazine issues itching to be read, for work purposes, of course. The dresses in today's stores were a total one-eighty from years ago. Now women wore colors, some more fashion-forward, some more revealing and some outright ridiculous.

I had just flipped to an article called - "Bridezillas and How To Tame Them"-when someone knocked at my door. I laid down my magazine so I could get up and answer it. Not the person I was expecting.

"Caleb? What are you doing here? Shouldn't you be enjoying yourself at the rehearsal dinner?" I asked.

"Thought I would take a break. If Janie's grandma pinches my butt one more time, I may lose it," he was serious, but I couldn't help giggling.

"An over-friendly old lady scares a big strong guy like you?" I chuckled.

"Keep on laughing. So, you think I'm strong, eh?" Caleb responded while showing off his muscles and waggling his eyebrows.

I stopped, and the warmth built in my cheeks. "That's not what I meant, well...yes, it is, but it's not the point."

Darn, he got me all flustered! Before I could come up with a good retort, my office door flew open. It was Adam, one of our servers.

"Hurry. It's Morgan. Nobody can find him, and Ms. Coleman is having a meltdown," he fretted.

Caleb and I rushed out, following the server to the event hall. Once we arrived, we found Janie out in the hallway, pacing back and forth while her parents attempted to calm her down.

"How could he do this to me?" she cried. "Doesn't he realize that this is one of the most important nights of my life? What are people going to think? Do you know how this looks? My fiancé ditches me at my rehearsal dinner. No, no, no!" She kept pacing, her arms flailing in the air as she ranted.

Maybe he got cold feet or changed his mind. Not that folks would blame him. I don't believe mentioning that right now would be helpful, though. Perhaps he just got stuck on his phone. He seemed glued to it most of the time anyway, so that wouldn't be out of the question.

I took charge, even though it was a struggle to remain composed. "Let's everyone just calm down, please. Can someone tell me exactly what's going on?"

Mrs. Coleman answered me first. "Janie wanted to start making toasts. When she went to retrieve Morgan, he wasn't anywhere to be found. She asked him to make the speeches early so they could get them done and enjoy the rest of the evening."

"I checked the hallway but didn't see him, then I looked out front, thinking he might have been on the phone, but he wasn't there either. His car is still in the parking lot," Mr. Coleman explained.

"About how long has it been since anyone has seen Morgan?" Caleb asked.

"Close to an hour by now. Last I saw, he was talking to Ted Banks and a couple of other people," the bride's father responded.

"I keep calling his cell phone, but it goes to voicemail!" Janie wailed. Her mom wrapped her arm around her and shushed her.

"What if we split up and look for him?" I suggested. "He can't be far away. Maybe he stepped into one of the other rooms to take a business call and lost track of time. I'm confident everything is fine, and he will feel sheepish about leaving his beautiful bride and his guests waiting." I managed a reassuring smile, hoping to allay their fears.

"Sounds like a great idea. Why don't Adam and I split up and search the perimeter and the parking lot," Caleb volunteered.

I turned to the bride's parents. "Mr. and Mrs. Coleman, will you stay here with Janie and keep the party going? No need to inform anyone just yet."

"Leah, I'll help as well." Meg offered.

"Great. Could you please start on this floor, and I will check downstairs. Then we can all meet back here in, say, fifteen, twenty minutes?" I asked.

Everyone agreed, and we split up to search. The Wedded Bliss wasn't so big, per se, but there was a lot of ground to cover.

I hated the basement. It had always freaked me out. Plus, the lighting left something to be desired. Before Aunt Sissy's passing, I constantly pestered her about hiring an electrician. After she died, I never found the time or funds to get around to it myself. We did have the foresight to keep a few flashlights handy by the stairs. I grabbed one before descending into the gloom.

As I shone the light around, it appeared to me everything was in order. Lots of storage boxes lined the two side walls, some more dusty than others. Once I reached the bottom, I was in the central area of the basement, able to view the smaller rooms on each side. We stored all our decorations and dishware down here.

I stood still and listened to see if I heard anything. Silence. I decided I would walk around counterclockwise for an orderly and thorough search of each room. Shining my flashlight high and low, I crept into the first one and found several boxes with silverware, dishes, and glassware. Nothing appeared out of place or recently moved. Several cobwebs and dust bunnies, but no Morgan. I left that one and shut the door behind me.

Next, I crossed to the right-side storage room doorway. Again, I entered and traveled in the same direction around space, checking over each section, still finding nothing. What a silly idea! Morgan would have no reason to ever come down here, but if it reassured Janie to check everywhere, I was going to do it.

Returning to the main area, I ventured into the last storage room. My light source sputtered. I smacked it a couple of times and then it crapped out. Moving more inward, I touched the wall to find the light switch. A few seconds later, it popped on, but it was very dim.

I trailed my fingers blindly along the wall and realized I had stepped into something sticky. Lifting my right foot, I wiped my hand across the bottom. Since the lighting was dim, it was hard to make out what I'd touched. I shook and smacked the flashlight, hoping it had a little more juice. It blinked on, and I held it over my hand, A cold finger of dread shot through me as I realized the substance was blood. I tracked the pool at my feet and found Morgan lying on his back, his eyes glazed over with a sword sticking out of his chest.

CHAPTER FOUR

My heart began racing, and my hands shook so badly. The bile rose in my throat as I fumbled for the flashlight. I felt woozy, but adrenaline kicked in, and I knew I had to get closer to him.

Leaning down, I reached out with my right hand to check and see if he had a pulse. I couldn't feel one, and he was cold to the touch. Help---I needed help. I bolted out of the room and flew up the stairs. My breathing became labored, and I gasped for air. I took a few much-needed moments to calm myself down before opening the door. Inside, I was screaming.

I hurried over to the side entrance to see if I could find Caleb or Meg. Neither was visible when I first stepped outside, so I took a chance and headed to the left. Trying not to alert any of the guests who may be near one of the windows, I walked calmly, then sped up until I reached another window, slowed down, then sped up again. Once I rounded the corner, I saw Caleb and Adam.

I rushed over to them. "Hurry, I found Morgan. Adam, can you call 911? I think it might be too late!" I hissed.

"Show me where he is, now!" Caleb grabbed my hand and dragged me towards the building.

"Wait!" I protested and spun around. "Adam, will you get Janie and her parents? Put them in the Heart Room. Once I take Caleb downstairs, I'll meet with them when I come back up."

"Yes, Ms. Jordan, right away," the server responded.

Caleb continued yanking me after him. He was going so fast, I almost fell.

Once we got inside, he looked over at me. "All right, where is he?"

I motioned for him to follow me to the basement door. We hustled down the stairs, and I pointed at the storage room. He entered while I waited. My heart was still racing, and my hands wouldn't stop shaking. I crossed my arms in an attempt to soothe myself. A few minutes later, he walked back out.

"Well?" I asked nervously.

His expression was grim as he shook his head. "Morgan's gone."

I squashed down my rising panic. "Who could do such a thing?"

Before I could finish my thoughts, several people came bustling down the steps. It was Meg, followed by Janie and her parents. My stomach fell.

"What is going on? Your server mentioned you were the one who found Morgan. Where is he?" Mr. Coleman demanded.

Caleb held out his hands in a vain attempt to calm them before he solemnly reported, "I hate to tell you this, but he is no longer with us."

"What do you mean? Dead? He was just fine two hours ago," the angry father of the bride exclaimed.

"We've contacted 911, and they should be arriving any minute. I'm terribly sorry for your loss," I expressed.

"What happened?" Morgan's fiancé asked and started to wail.

"We're not sure, but it's probably best we wait for the authorities before any assumptions are made," Caleb spoke up.

"This is despicable! How dare someone ruin my princess's special day? Just what kind of business are you running here, Ms. Jordan, where your clients get killed?"

"Mr. Coleman, this has never happened in all of The Wedded Bliss's history! We'll do everything in our power to cooperate with law enforcement and see that justice is served," I promised, hoping to appeal to his sense of decency.

"Don't you worry, you'll be hearing from my lawyers! Elizabeth, let's take our daughter upstairs. No need for her to witness any more of this tragedy," the angry man grumbled.

"Yes, dear," his wife responded as she trailed behind her husband.

"I'm confident this can be dealt with in a more peaceful manner," Caleb offered.

"Tell that to my devastated daughter!" Mr. Coleman barked over his shoulder as they escorted a sobbing Janie up the stairs.

"Leah, why don't you go, too? Keep an eye out for the ambulance and police, then guide them down here. We need to make sure no one leaves," Caleb suggested.

If it had been any other situation, I would have questioned him on how he could stay so calm, but now was not that time. Heading back upstairs, I went outside to direct the emergency personnel. Barely five minutes passed when a few police cruisers, an ambulance and two fire trucks arrived. An officer exited his car and approached me while another followed behind.

"Ma'am are you the individual who called us about an injured person?" he asked. The badge on his chest said Sergeant Patterson.

"No sir, it was an employee of mine, but I am Leah Jordan, the owner here at The Wedded Bliss. I can take you to the victim," I responded.

"Great. Fisher, you stay here and start cordoning off the area. I've already called in the detective, and he's bringing the crime scene kit. No one leaves, and no one comes in, no matter what," Sergeant Patterson ordered.

"Yes, sir," he replied as he headed back to his cruiser.

"Ma'am, if you would please show me where the victim is located," the officer requested.

"Of course." I for him to follow me inside.

We made our way through to the basement door with him at my heels. As we reached the bottom of the stairs, I pointed toward the storage room. He went in, and a couple of minutes later, Caleb came out and joined me.

"The officer told me I needed to come out so I wouldn't contaminate the crime scene any further. How are you doing?" he asked.

"A little better. At least I stopped shaking." I held my hand out to demonstrate.

"Good, I'm glad. He said to wait upstairs until he came up. He wants to take statements from everyone, especially you since you found Morgan."

"How are you so calm during all of this?" I asked. "Maybe it is because you're from a bigger city, but murder isn't exactly an everyday occurrence in Ashford."

"Let's follow their orders, and I'll explain."

Once we were upstairs, more police officers had arrived. A couple of them were escorting people to separate rooms, while the others guarded the exits and entrances. We were directed to the Love Room, which happened to be empty. After the officer left, I turned to Caleb and asked him to start explaining.

"As far as everyone is concerned, I'm just one of the groomsmen. My true role is a private investigator who also offers security services. Mr. Coleman has received some minor threats since before the engagement was announced and Morgan had been acting strange, so Janie brought me on board to investigate. A few more of my men will be here on the wedding day."

Mind blown. "Why wouldn't she have mentioned anything to me before now?"

"She didn't want her fiancé or her father to be so stressed, so she decided to hire me to help figure out what was going on and keep them out of the loop. It was my idea to be a part of the wedding party so I could be as close as possible. I'm an 'old friend' of Janie's from back in the day who is like a 'brother' to her. She reached out via my website to hire me, and we handled everything online."

Hmm, so Caleb really wasn't a friend of theirs. It made sense how he stayed so calm when we found Morgan's body. But that was beside the point right now. "Is there anything else I should know?"

"I am also a former detective with the Putnam Ridge Township Police. About five years ago, I was involved in a dangerous pursuit, got injured and left the force." He shrugged.

My eyes widened. Wait, what? A cop, too? "A high-speed chase? Like what they show on television and in the movies?"

"My partner and I were chasing a suspect when he lost control and slammed into our cruiser, trying to get away. My left leg was pinned under the dashboard in the crash, which shattered my femur. Once I arrived at the hospital, the doctors realized just how bad it was. I lost a lot of blood, and it was touch and go at first. A steel rod and several months of physical and occupational therapy later, I was able to walk again. When I came back to the force, they stuck me at a desk job, which I loathed. So, I took an early retirement and decided to work for myself," Caleb explained.

My mind was going a million miles a minute. The handsome investigator wasn't just a groomsman. I found the dead body of one of our clients in The Wedded Bliss basement and now cops and detectives had invaded. I felt like I was in a bad dream or some kind of multiverse. "Is there anything we need to do?"

"If I could meet with you and get more information on the facility, the staff, et cetera, that would be great. It's even more imperative after this evening's events," he urged.

Before I could ask more questions, another officer entered and escorted us to separate rooms down the hall. I ended up being taken to Meg's office near mine and Chelsea's. He told me to take a seat and someone would be in to speak with me. As I waited, my mind began swirling. With all the people that attended the party, who would want to hurt Morgan?

Twenty minutes later, there was a knock on the door and Sargeant Patterson came in.

"Ms. Jordan, I'd like to talk to you about what happened here tonight. What you may have heard, what you saw, and anything suspicious." He took the chair across from me at the desk and pulled out a notebook.

"Am I under arrest?" It wasn't exactly a common occurrence for me to be talking to an officer. The only crime in my life included a couple of speeding tickets and punching Eddie Beck on the playground in fourth grade because he wouldn't stop pulling on my pigtails.

"Not currently, ma'am. We are conducting preliminary interviews with everyone who was here this evening. That way, we can begin to piece together what happened tonight. Now that doesn't mean we may not have to call you back in for further questioning at a later time." He tapped his pen on the notebook and opened it up. "Let's get started. Please state your full name, date of birth, and address."

"Leah Elizabeth Jordan, April 12th, 1983. My address is 5674 Castle Drive, Ashford, Ohio," I responded.

"Ms. Jordan, can you start from the beginning of your day and tell me what occurred?"

"I woke up around 6:30 a.m., fed my cats, got dressed, ran a few errands in town, and headed to the office. I always like to get there early prior to an event and make sure things are running smoothly," I answered.

"Was Mr. Vanderbilt there when you arrived? What time did you get to The Wedded Bliss?" he asked.

"No, he was not. Just the kitchen, catering staff, and myself. I believe it was four. The engagement party was to begin at six-thirty."

"How did you know the victim?"

"He and his fiancée, Janie Coleman, hired me as their wedding planner."

"When did you meet them?"

"I think our first meeting was in December 2013."

"How much interaction did you have with the deceased?" the officer questioned.

"Not a lot, the typical amount a groom is involved. Mostly I dealt with the bride. He was there for the initial appointment and some of the follow-up meetings for the wedding, rehearsal dinner and engagement party."

"Have you ever had any problems with them?"

"Not really. We did have a recent issue over a bill, but we were able to get that resolved," I answered.

He raised an eyebrow and looked up from his notepad. "Do you believe it is settled? How can you be so sure?"

"Chelsea was working to resolve that; she is the financial person and one of my business partners at The Wedded Bliss."

"Chelsea...what's Chelsea's last name?"

"Baker."

"So, where were you when the engagement party began?"

"I was in my office trying to catch up on some client files and paperwork."

"Do you remember when you learned the victim was missing?"

"I believe it was close to nine-forty-five. According to Adam, one of our employees, Mr. Vanderbilt hadn't been seen for an hour. I was talking with Caleb Hamilton at the time when we were notified. His fiancée was upset, so a few of us decided to split up and search."

"You went downstairs alone?"

"Yes sir. I know the building layout exceptionally well, so I volunteered while the others spread out.

The sergeant became more attentive. "When you reached it, did anything seem unusual?"

"No. The lighting is not the greatest down there, but it appeared normal."

"Did you see, hear, or smell something peculiar?"

"No, sir. The only person I saw was Morgan, er, Mr. Vanderbilt," I replied, stumbling over my words.

He looked up at me. "Did you touch anything?"

I nodded. "The doorknobs and Mr. Vanderbilt when I checked for a pulse."

He cleared his throat and sat up straighter. "Is there anything else that might be pertinent to this investigation?"

"No, sir." As much as I racked my brain, I could think of nothing. Whether it was shock or stress, my mind was all jumbled.

"I think that will be all. Thank you, Ms. Jordan, for your time." Sergeant Patterson handed me his business card. "If you remember something in regard to the case, please contact me."

"Thank you." I took it from him and held it in my hand. "What happens now?"

"We should finish our interviews in a few hours. Once the coroner has finished and the crime scene unit has cleared the area, you can lock up the building. If they need more time to collect evidence or investigate, then you may not be able to enter the basement until they are done.

"Will we still have access to our offices?"

"I don't anticipate that being a problem. Now, if you'll excuse me, I have more witnesses I must speak with." He ushered me to the door and held it open as I passed by.

Back in the hallway, guests and officers lingered. I glanced around to see if I could spot Caleb, but I was unable to locate him. After searching for a few more minutes, I decided to return to my office.

"Leah! There you are!" Chelsea called out as she rushed over to me. An officer was close behind her.

"Ma'am, you need to get back here! Stop!" the policeman yelled as he caught up to us.

"What are you doing here?" I asked her.

"I heard on the police scanner that something was going on. I arrived as fast as I could. These buffoons wouldn't listen to me when I told them who I was." She gave the cop a dirty look. "They refused to let me in, so I caught one of them off guard and forced my way through."

"Oh, you didn't!" I gasped.

She was not a person who sat around twiddling her thumbs. If someone she cared about was in danger of any kind, she would be right there.

The policeman cleared his throat. "Ma'am! I really need you to come with me. You are trespassing in an official crime scene!" he exclaimed.

Chelsea snapped her head around. "Excuse me? I am talking to my best friend, who also happens to be the owner of this business. She'll vouch for me. I work here too." She looked over at me.

I nodded in confirmation. "She's correct. Chelsea is an employee here."

He looked at both of us and furrowed his brows. "

Another officer approached us. "Watson, there you are. The lieutenant has been looking for you. C'mon!"

Chelsea smiled at the new officer. "Hey Matty, long time to see!"

He blushed. "Hey Chels. Crazy night."

"Fine. Let's go," Watson grumbled.

They both walked back down the hall towards the lobby.

"Whew, that was nuts. I'll ask you again, what are you doing here? I thought you were out with Brad, er Brayden. Whatever the name is of the newest flavor of the week." I laughed.

Chelsea rolled her eyes. "Haha. So funny. I thought you could be hurt. I had to come to see for myself. Where is Meg?"

"She left after she got questioned. I was afraid all the stress would be too much on her and the baby. Thank God you're here. I appreciate it. I just can't believe this has happened."

"What exactly is going on? I saw all the cruisers and equipment out front. The radio mentioned a serious accident?" Chelsea asked.

"It's more than that. Someone's been m-murdered." I stumbled over the word.

Her mouth dropped open, and she shook her head in disbelief. "No! What? Here? Who? Nothing happens here in Ashford except for some graffiti, petty theft and Old Man Winters, who falls asleep in the town gazebo after an all-night bender."

Sadly, she was right.

"Not anymore, I guess. Morgan went missing from the party earlier and when he couldn't be found, a few of us spread out to look, and that's when I discovered him. No one knows exactly what happened. The police are still conducting interviews and collecting evidence. It will be some time before they finish." I explained.

"Whoa, Mr. Cocky? I better contact Lou at his law office," Chelsea muttered.

"Good idea. Mr. Coleman is very upset. He already threatened to sue." I rubbed my forehead where a stress headache started to throb. "If he does, what are we going to do?"

Chelsea put her hands out. "Now, now, just calm down. Let's not jump to conclusions yet. Let me call Lou and get his advice. I am sure he was just speaking out in the heat of the moment and didn't mean it. Then we can go from there. It's not like there is an instruction manual on how to deal with a murder in your place of business."

I released a deep breath. "You know, you're right. I've already been interviewed. I'm going to my office and let the authorities do their jobs. You may want to find one of the officers, apologize for your earlier antics, and answer their questions. They are interested in speaking to everyone who knew the victim or had contact with him. "

"Good idea. The sooner they get their questioning done. The sooner they can be out of our hair. What are we going to do about everything for the wedding tomorrow?" Chelsea asked.

"I'm not sure. Maybe after he has some time to cool down, Mr. Coleman will be easier to speak to, and we can discuss it then."

"Let's hope. I'll go and speak with an officer and come find you when we're finished." She walked away.

I continued down the hallway to my office. Tonight was definitely a 'WWASD' moment! There have been some feuding family members, heated mothers of the bride, and some drunk and disorderly guests, but never a homicide.

Once inside, I plopped down on my desk chair. What a long, long day. To pass the time, I decided to make copies of my records just in case the police requested them. My mind kept turning and churning, trying to figure out who might have had something against Morgan. Not necessarily the most pleasant guy, but no one deserved to be murdered, especially the night before their wedding.

Twenty-five minutes later, I had copied all the paperwork from our file for Janie and Morgan. Placing the duplicates in a new manila folder, I set it in the upper left drawer of my desk. Nothing more I could do right now until I heard from the authorities.

Grabbing my purse and jacket, I shut off the lights and closed the door as I stepped into the hallway. I noticed most of the guests and a majority of the police officers had dispersed as well. Sergeant Patterson stood at the end of the hall, staring at his notes.

"May I have a moment, sir?" I inquired as I approached him.

He looked up. "Yes, what can I help you with?"

"Have you been able to collect everything you needed? Have all the guests left?" I asked.

"Ma'am, you can't rush an investigation. Consider The Wedded Bliss closed until further notice."

"What am I supposed to tell my clients?"

"The truth, Ms. Jordan." And with that, he walked away.

CHAPTER FIVE

My obnoxious alarm roused me out of a cozy slumber and thrust me back into a harsh reality. I pulled the covers over my head like I used to do when I was a child in the hopes that last night's tragic events were all just a terrible nightmare. In my heart of hearts, I knew it wasn't, so I flung off the covers and dragged myself out of bed to face the day. I left the cats snuggled together in the comforter as I made my way to the kitchen for a glass of apple juice. Their blissful ignorance sparked a pang of envy in me.

When I padded out to the porch to retrieve the morning paper, my stomach sank. There it was splashed all over the front page of the Ashford Chronicle, 'Local Socialite's Husband to Be, Murdered'.

A picture of Morgan was plastered on the cover, along with an engagement photo of him and Janie. Additionally, they had included ones from The Wedded Bliss roped off with crime scene tape. A downfall of living in a small town. When anything happened, it made headline news, and murder was a huge story. Before the day concluded, everyone would be speculating about what took place. I really hoped they would catch the killer soon.

After skimming through the rest of the newspaper, I figured I'd better get ready for work. However, the dread I felt at having to deal with the aftermath of the killing descended upon me and threatened to suffocate me. I turned the water pressure up in the shower and stood under it until it ran cold, hoping it would blast some life back into my body.

I put on the pair of tan pants and a navy, short-sleeved top I laid out. Fifteen minutes later, I was finally refreshed and ready to take on the new day. My priority was to head over to The Wedded Bliss and figure out a game plan. Chelsea already texted me to let me know she was on the way to the office.

Seeing the building after all the crime tape, police cars and officers that were present the previous night felt weird. It was such a haven for me. A place of happiness, of new beginnings, and of a future to come. Only one cruiser waited in the lot. I exited my car and went over to speak with him.

"Greetings, ma'am," he said after rolling down his window and sticking out his hand. "I'm Officer Michaels."

I shook it. "Morning, sir. Am I able to work in the building now?"

"Yes, they cleared the scene hours ago after the last investigator left. I was ordered to stand guard until you arrived," he responded.

"I appreciate that. Is there anything I need to do?"

"Not really. Sergeant Patterson said he would be in touch. We do advise that you contact a clean-up team to assist with decontaminating and sterilizing the area before using it again."

"Thank you, officer. I'll do that."

"You are welcome. I am going to leave now. Have a good day." He saluted and drove off.

After I made sure he was out of the parking lot, I unlocked the front door and stepped inside, locking it behind me. The kind policeman's demeanor eased my anxiety a very tiny bit. I decided just to until Chelsea arrived.

Ten minutes later, she knocked and came in, tossing her purse and laptop bag in one of the chairs across my desk while she flopped into the other and heaved a tremendous sigh.

"And a good morning to you, too," I chuckled.

"Hello," she responded.

"What's wrong with you, woman?"

She appeared completely drained. Her normally neat, straight hair was frizzy and thrown back into a messy ponytail.

"I'm exhausted. I didn't get done until almost 1 A.M," she replied.

"Really? Why?"

"After my little 'incident' last night, they weren't in a hurry to question me. I had to wait until everyone else was finished, then they interviewed me."

I sighed, "Oh Chelsea, what am I going to do with you? Other than that, how did it go?"

She let out a deep breath and pushed back a stray lock of hair that fell into her eyes. "It was fine, the basics. What do you know? Where were you when it happened? Did you have any problems with the victim?"

"Okay, good. I am sure they just had to be thorough," I said.

"True, it's their job. However, I may have told them a little more than I should have," Chelsea grimaced.

I raised my eyebrows. "Too much?"

"You know how I can go on and on sometimes when I'm stressed or tired. The more we talked about Morgan, the more I kept thinking about what a jerk he's been to me and that day when he and Janie burst in and went off about the bill."

"Oh, you didn't!" I exclaimed. "Now they'll think you had a motive and see you as a potential suspect."

Chelsea scoffed and rolled her eyes. "You have been watching too much television. Leah, I couldn't hurt a fly. You know me. It was a stupid mistake.

I wasn't thinking straight. A little tiff with an obnoxious client is not a big deal."

"Have you talked to Lou?"

She nodded. "Yes, I spoke with him this morning before I came over."

"What were you able to find out?"

"There is bad and good news."

I didn't like the sound of that. "What's the good news?"

"He will review our errors and omissions policy. He feels there should be no ill effect on The Wedded Bliss."

"That's comforting. And the bad news?" I sucked in a deep breath.

"He received a call from Winston Fordham, an attorney representing Janie Coleman and her family."

"Ugh. Really?"

"Apparently, Mr. Coleman's threat wasn't so empty after all. He's filing a suit against The Wedded Bliss.

Oh, no. My stomach dropped. "What do we do?"

"Right now, we wait. Lou said not to worry yet, it may just be Mr. Coleman blowing off steam. He needs someone to blame, and we just happen to be the targets," Chelsea explained.

This was not good. Not good at all. "It could ruin us. He has a lot of pull in the community."

A look of concern came over her face. "Leah, it was an accident. We had no idea it was going to happen, and we had no hand in causing it. Emotions are running high, and once the case is solved and the killer is caught, things will go back to normal."

"I guess you're right. It's just nerve-wracking," I sighed.

"Slight topic change. Do you mind coming with me to the Cupid Room?" she inquired.

I shrugged my shoulders. "Sure."

We headed down the hall and entered. It was as if time stood still. Everything was set up as it had been for the rehearsal dinner.

"Eerie, isn't it?" Chelsea asked as she turned to look at me.

I nodded as my eyes scanned the room. "It's sad too. I'll have the staff go in tomorrow and finish cleaning it out. Any items that don't belong to us will be boxed up and we'll arrange for someone to come pick them up."

"Let's get out of here for now. You promised to tell me more about what happened last night," she stated as she motioned towards the door. "Did you also have time to discuss the new 'Bride on a Budget' packages? I'd love to see what you've developed. "

"Let me just ask Steve about cleaning this room, and I can meet you in my office, say, in five minutes?" I replied.

"Perfect," Chelsea said before she left.

I sat down at my desk and sent an email, then pulled out my notes on the new packages. She popped in a few moments later.

"Start from the beginning. What the heck happened?" she asked.

I leaned back in my chair. "I came in early like I always do before an event, checked in with Chef Stefan and the wait staff. Everything was under control. Janie, Morgan, and her parents had arrived, and they began greeting guests. I excused myself and retreated to my office."

"How did you find out he was missing?"

"Actually, a couple hours after it started, Caleb stopped by." I felt my face get warm.

Chelsea waggled her eyebrows. "Ooh...what was that all about?"

I groaned. "Now, get your mind out of the gutter. He wanted a place to hide away from Janie's grandmother and her shenanigans. We were just shooting the breeze when Adam knocked on my door and explained Morgan was missing and that we needed to come quick because his fiancée was having a major meltdown."

Chelsea waved her hand in a rolling motion. "Go on."

"The three of us hurried back to the Cupid Room and found Janie and her parents and a couple of groomsmen standing in the hallway. Morgan hadn't been seen in quite some time, so I asked them to stay with her while some of us searched for the missing man. I headed to the lower level, Caleb and Adam went outside, and Meg took the first floor."

"You ventured into that terrifying basement by yourself? What were you thinking?" she gasped.

I recounted the events leading up to the gruesome discovery.

"Oh. My. God. What did you do?"

"Once the screaming inside my head subsided, I ran upstairs and outside to find Caleb and Adam. I asked our server to call 911, and we waited for them to show up."

"You were certain he was...gone?"

"Yes, I led Caleb to the room. He felt for a pulse, but there was none." I shuddered.

"What did the cops say?"

"They were in a hurry to get the building secure and make sure no one left. Then the lead officer asked his men to break the guests, staff, etc. into smaller groups to be interviewed."

Chelsea's eyes widened. "Wow, it must have been chaos!"

"That is an understatement. However, the officers moved quickly and had everyone sorted in no time. When you saw me, I had just gotten done being questioned."

"Mine felt like it took forever. I didn't know what to say."

I looked directly at her. "The truth, Chelsea."

"I mean, I did, but they seemed to be really stuck on the fact that my alibi stunk and kept harping on the disagreement between Morgan and me," she explained.

"About the bill?" I asked.

She nodded. "Yes. I told them it was resolved."

"Yeah, that's weird."

"After what felt like days, they finally let me go," Chelsea said, letting out a deep breath.

"Good. We really should discuss what to do now. How do we handle this? I don't want us to be known as the place where grooms come to die. We're trying to bring business in, not scare it away," I moaned.

"Exactly. Therefore, we need to focus on what we can do. Remain positive."

"You're right. Maybe these new plans will help. Here you go." I slid them across the desk.

"I can look them over and..." Chelsea's voice trailed off as two police officers entered my office with Sally trailing right behind.

Our secretary was visibly upset. "I'm sorry, Leah. I tried to get them to stay out front, but they insisted they couldn't wait.

"Good afternoon," the taller policeman said. The badge listed his last name as Thompson.

"Ma'am," the shorter official stated, tipping his hat.

Officer Thompson stuck his thumbs down into his utility belt. "We're looking for Ms. Baker."

Chelsea sat up straighter in her chair. "I'm Ms. Baker. What is this regarding?"

"We have a warrant for your arrest, for the murder of Morgan Vanderbilt. If you could, please stand up," he directed.

"What's going on? I answered your questions. I told you I have no idea what happened to him!" My best friend shot me a frantic glance. "Leah, what do I do?"

I put my finger up to my lips. "Chelsea don't say anything else. This is a huge mistake. Just try to remain calm. I'll call Lou at his office, and he'll get all this straightened out."

The arresting officer cleared his throat. "While I appreciate your concern, we need to transport Ms. Baker to the station."

"What evidence do you have against her? Could you please tell us that?" I questioned.

"I can't disclose that information at this time. You can come down in a few hours and speak to the sergeant on duty after she has been booked and processed," he replied.

The second policeman, Kurtis, instructed Chelsea to put her hands behind her back and placed a handcuff on each of her wrists. The officers pushed past me with her in tow and out the door. Officer Thompson handed me a business card, then made a little note in his notebook before placing it in his pocket. Sally and I followed them outside.

It was so awful seeing the fear and confusion on our friend's face. "Does she really need to be handcuffed?"

"It's protocol," he replied.

"Not as dramatic or cool as in the crime dramas on television." Chelsea tried cracking a joke. "Don't worry about me. Just call Lou," she called out from the cruiser as Officer Kurtis placed her inside.

Still in shock after Chelsea's arrest, I managed to make the somber drive over to the Breckenridge County Jail. Our government annex served many purposes. It also housed the Ashford Police Department, the courthouse, the mayor's office and a small morgue. I waited a very long three hours before I drove over because I couldn't wait a minute more.

I lucked out and found a parking spot in the square. Exiting my car, I snatched my purse and took the stairs up to the government building. The police station and jail were located at the lower level. To my right, at the bottom, was an officer and a metal detector that everyone had to pass through.

I picked up one of the baskets and placed my keys and sunglasses in it, then I handed my purse over too. He motioned for me to step on through. Making it past with no issues, the guard returned my things. I quickly put my items back in my pocket and went downstairs to the police station. I entered the double glass doors and approached the desk.

"Ma'am, can I help you?" he asked with a smile. Officer Garcia was blessed with silky, dark-brown hair, green eyes, and a flawless olive complexion.

He almost made me forget why I was there.

"Ma'am?" he prompted.

I blinked and found my voice. "Yes, I'm here to speak with Chelsea Baker, please."

"All right, sign in on this log. I will need to see your identification, and you have to leave your belongings with me. Once you are finished with your visit, you can come back for them," he instructed.

The handsome officer slid the logbook closer to me, and I gave him my driver's license. Once I signed my name, I handed over my purse and pocket contents to him.

"Is there anything else?" I asked.

"You will have twenty minutes. It is required that you enter the room and sit at a table the officer inside directs you to. Then the inmate you are visiting is brought out. Absolutely no touching and hands must always be kept above where they are visible. When time is up, the individual is escorted back to their cell, and you are permitted to leave. Return to the desk, sign out, and retrieve your items."

I nodded. "I understand."

"Leah?"

When I turned to see who called my name, I noticed Luke standing there.

Luke Strickland was Meg's older brother. We had known each other since his sister and I met in third grade. Meg, Chelsea and I enjoyed spying on him as kids. He saw us as annoying geeks. He played sports and was part of the popular crowd. He was also the first guy I had a crush on.

His blonde hair was short but longer on the top and his eyes were so blue, it was like looking at mini oceans where all you could see was water for miles. He had an oval face with just a little scruff. The uniform shirt accented his broad shoulders and showed off his muscles. Time had treated him well.

"Oh, hi," I said, trying to sound casual.

"What are you doing here?" he asked.

"You haven't heard? Chelsea was arrested!" I blurted.

"I knew that was a possibility. I'm sorry to hear that," Luke replied.

"How could you think that? You know wouldn't hurt a fly! You have the wrong person."

"Leah, we are just doing our jobs."

"You've known Chelsea for years. This isn't right," I grumbled.

"Again, I apologize. If we're mistaken, then the truth will come out. Let us work this investigation," Luke urged.

Before I could respond, Officer Smiley came out from behind the desk. "Ms. Jordan, if you'll please head to the left and wait, I am going to allow you entry."

Fuming, I stood at the door as directed until it buzzed. I grabbed the handle and yanked it open. There was another door. Once the first one closed, there was yet another buzz, allowing me to go through the second. On the opposite side, a separate officer waited, and the visitation area was to my right. He pointed me to a round table in the middle with two seats.

The room itself was sizable. The walls were a stark white, the tables and chairs were out of the 70s and 80s and could have really used an update. I sat with my hands clasped on top, trying to find something to occupy my frantic brain while I waited for them to bring out my friend. Yeah, I had nothing.

The door at the far end opened, and an officer escorted her in.

"Just remember, you only have twenty minutes," he reminded us and took up his post across the room.

"Oh, Chelsea! Are you okay?" I asked as she sat down.

She gave me a half-smile and shrugged her shoulders. "I'm fine. I'm a tough cookie. Never thought I would be here, but it's not that bad."

I huffed. "You shouldn't be here at all. They are going off assumptions and have completely misconstrued the disagreement with Morgan, making it into something more than it was."

"They did, but it is what it is. I guess my alibi is in question. We know the truth and soon they will too," she assured me.

"What if they don't? I can't just do nothing. If we were in opposite positions, you wouldn't sit idly by," I grumbled.

"What are you saying?" Chelsea asked.

"We're going to investigate on our own. The sooner they find the real killer, the sooner you can clear your name, and we can get back to business. The Coleman family is offering a large reward for anyone who brings the murderer to justice. Think of how we could use that to turn things around at The Wedded Bliss! Plus, if Mr. Coleman really does file a lawsuit against us, and we solve it, he would have no choice but to drop it."

"I see your point, but that's what the police are for. Just let them do their job."

I couldn't believe she wasn't agreeing with me! "But what do we have to lose?"

She studied my face. "What if investigating is too risky? You don't have a clue about how to protect yourself, and if you get too involved, you could end up being the next victim."

I held my right hand up. "I promise that if it becomes unsafe, I'll reach out to the police."

She shook her head. "I'm not sure if this is a good idea. Do you even know the first thing about investigating a crime?"

"Not exactly, but I'll figure it out as I go along. You are innocent, and I am determined to prove it. We're best friends, and I will always be there for you."

"I really appreciate that. I'd do the same for you."

"You're my family, Chelsea, and family sticks together through thick and thin. I'll contact Lou after I leave and see if I can get an update on your arrest and what happens next. Knowing him, he'll have you out in no time."

"Thank you, Leah, I owe you," she reached across to squeeze my hand.

"No touching!" the officer bellowed. We both jerked our hands back as if we were caught sneaking in the cookie jar. "Visiting is over. Please head towards the exit."

"Be strong. Everything will work out," I said, hoping to reassure her.

"I am going to. Talk to you soon," Chelsea replied.

I rose and turned toward the door. The officer had already come to retrieve her.

"Wait, Leah, do me one more favor?"

I turned back around. "Sure. What do you need?"

"Can you please go over to my house and feed Mr. Charlie?"

"Of course."

Mr. Charlie was Chelsea's fish. The only animal she was willing to make time for — he was the goldfish that just wouldn't die.

I left the visitors' room and waited to be buzzed through the two sets of doors. Heading straight to the desk, I picked up my belongings and made sure to get my driver's license back. It was awful seeing my best friend behind bars. To consider her a suspect and arrest her based on a disagreement was ridiculous. It was as if they didn't even think about anyone else. Either they were incompetent, lazy, or getting pressured to take someone into custody.

I knew I assured Chelsea I would go to the police if things got hard, but I would not sit idly by and let her be arrested for a crime she didn't commit. I refused to wait for someone else to unravel the puzzle. Working at The Wedded Bliss taught me how to coax all types of people into opening up and trusting me. I intended to find the real murderer and bring them to justice, and I had better get started.

CHAPTER SIX

With all the chaos making my nerves a wreck, I decided to stop by my house and visit the fur babies for some emotional therapy. If nothing else, I could really use some TLC. Who is better than an animal to give you unconditional love? I parked my car and walked to the front door. Two little furry faces popped through the mini blinds. It was like they knew their mommy was home. Once I made it inside, they took turns meowing and doing figure eights around my legs.

"Hello ladies, you didn't miss me, did you?" I cooed.

Oreo looked up at me and meowed.

Setting my keys and purse on the table in the foyer, I went into the living room and kicked my shoes off. I climbed onto the couch, tossed the blanket over me, and let the pair of therapists get settled at my feet.

My mind drifted off, and I slipped into quite a dream. My parents, Aunt Sissy and Chelsea were all there with me at a church. It was my special day. My groom and I came out and descended the church steps as the bells began to ring.

Wait, those weren't in my dreams, that was my doorbell. Sighing, I flung off the cover and hopped up to answer the door. I cracked it open and found myself staring out at a nice-looking gentleman in a nondescript brown uniform holding a clipboard.

"Ms. Jordan?"

I wondered what he was selling.

"I'm sorry, but no solicitors. Didn't you see the sign?" I pointed to the sticker on the window on the left side that clearly stated 'No Solicitors'.

"Ma'am, I'm just here to deliver a letter. This is for you." He handed it to me.

The envelope was plain white. It wasn't particularly easy to make out a name, or sender as the printing was smudged. Turning it over in my hand, I tested its weight. It felt very light.

"Okay, thank you? Do I need to sign something?"

I looked back up at him, but he had already made it halfway down my front steps.

As he reached the bottom, he turned around.

"You've been served," he said, continuing a quick pace down the sidewalk toward a plain, blue, two-door sedan.

He got in, started it up, and sped off. Son of a gun! I was so stunned. I didn't remember going inside. I just kept staring at the envelope, as I tried to decide whether to open it or not.

After much thought and freaking out, I figured the best course of action was to take it with me to Lou's. I needed to talk to him about Chelsea too, so I might as well kill two birds with one stone.

Lou Little's law office was located in downtown Ashford - if you could even call it 'downtown'. Several of the buildings were original and had seen better days. Navigating the one-way streets around the town square, I found a parking spot just past his front door.

Patty, his long-time secretary, sat behind the desk, pecking away at her keyboard with one hand while holding the phone to her ear with the other. She gave a finger wave when I entered and motioned for me to take a seat in the cozy waiting room. I only had to wait a few minutes before she was done.

"Hey, sweetie! To what do we owe this pleasure?" she gushed, coming around her desk to hug me.

"Morning, Patty. Is Lou available?" I asked as I returned her embrace.

"And here I thought you were here to see me," she teased and returned to her chair. "I think he's still here. Let me check for you. I was so sorry to hear about your friend. There is no way a girl as nice as she is could have done something so awful. Rumor on the grapevine says that Morgan deserved what was coming and more!" She quickly covered her mouth. "Oh, just listen to me, a little old lady going on and on like a gossip monger. You shouldn't speak ill of the dead either." She looked down and clicked away on her keyboard.

A shudder went through my body. I still couldn't get the image of Morgan's lifeless body out of my head. I decided not to comment and brought the conversation back to the reason for my visit. "So, is Lou busy?"

"No. He just got off the phone. You can go to his office."

"Thank you!" I walked down the hallway and stopped at the attorney's door. It was slightly ajar, so I knocked first.

"Come on in," his deep voice called out.

I walked in and closed it behind me.

"Have a seat, Leah. What's going on?" He stood up as I came in and motioned for me to sit across from him.

I didn't waste time. "A few things. Originally, I wanted to come over and discuss the case against Chelsea, but another pressing matter has arisen."

"Not a problem. Let's start with your best friend. It's a quick update. As of right now, they don't have any solid evidence to hold her more than the thirty-six hours they are allowed. Then they either have to charge her or let her go. Everything they have is circumstantial and doesn't have a tie to her directly. I'm working my hardest to get her released as soon as possible."

"You know she and I both appreciate that. She is one of my right-hands, best friends, my family and I would be lost without her." I bit my lip and tried not to cry.

He reached across the desk and squeezed my hand.

"It's going to be fine. It will all work itself out," he assured me. "Now you mentioned there is something else you need to discuss?"

I reached into my purse and pulled out the envelope that was served earlier and handed it over to him. He took the papers out, unfolded them, and began reading to himself.

He scoffed, "This is ridiculous. The man is trying to sue for emotional damages and trauma withstood by his daughter due to the murder of her fiancé. I cannot see any valid merit to this case. Why don't you give me a couple of days to really look this over with a fine-toothed comb and determine if there are any loopholes? Worry about Chelsea right now. I'll contact you when I have something." Lou reached across the table again and squeezed my hand.

I felt a little better knowing he had our best interests at heart. I was even more motivated now to figure out who did this and bring them to justice.

When I left his office, I went straight for my own. Another day, another dollar. I wished that was so. Our phones had hardly rung except for nosy people asking about the murder and wanting to tour the crime scene. Gruesome busybodies!

I opened my laptop and pressed the power button. While I waited for it to come to life, my stomach let out a ravenous growl. The day was already emotionally draining, and I realized I hadn't eaten yet. I opened my browser and searched for Pete's pizza so I could order an Italian sub, no tomatoes and a side salad with ranch dressing.

I decided to start making notes. I plucked out a fresh legal pad from my desk drawer. Writing Morgan's name at the top, I underlined it. Then I wrote down what I knew about him already. Unfortunately, it wasn't much.

I pulled out the Vanderbilt/Coleman file folder from the filing cabinet and scanned the information sheet, I believed his employer was listed. Bingo! Marketing executive at Coleman Industries. Why was I not surprised? His address was 5275 Laymen Drive in the Ashford Estates, which was a fairly new, upscale neighborhood filled with pricey condominiums on the north side of town.

My eyes skimmed the rest of the sheet. There were work and cell phone numbers but no contact details for his family. He'd only provided their names. We always asked for both sets of parent's information in case any emergencies or unexpected issues arose. Weird. Why hadn't I caught that before? I made a little notation on my notepad.

Now that I had everything written down, what about social media? Who didn't have Facebook, Twitter or Instagram in this day and age? I went back to the search engine and typed in Morgan's name. A profile popped up in the results, and I clicked on it. It was surprisingly plain. His main photo was one of him and his fiancée. I continued to scroll, but there wasn't much else except the basic information and random memes he shared.

Janie mentioned something in our initial consultation that he had only lived in Ashford for a few years. Momentarily stumped, I decided to shift my focus and concentrate on her. I flipped to a new page in my notepad and wrote her name on the top.

Maybe I could create a timeline of the couple's relationship. The easiest way, of course, would be talking to the former bride to be. However, her father made that complicated at the moment by filing a lawsuit against us.

Small towns thrived on gossip, and the society pages were full of information, local events and pictures. I turned the pad sideways, went to the next blank page and drew a horizontal line down the middle. On the right, I wrote 'got engaged'.

Next, I thought about those closest to the victim. Janie sat at the top of the list. She did suspect things were going on with Morgan. Maybe she found something out or cracked from all the stress of the wedding? Although she did seem genuinely devastated, the whole clueless socialite thing could all be an act. It was something to keep in mind. I added the bride's parents, the bridal party and everyone else present at the rehearsal dinner. That was only seventy-five to a hundred people, give or take a few. I sighed.

Speaking with her parents would be important, though right now might not be the best time. Morgan's groomsmen would be a good start. Besides Caleb, there were three more, Logan, Evan, and Cody. Most of them had known Morgan for years. I just needed to track them down.

Before I could start writing a list of other tasks to accomplish, the front doorbell rang. Looking up at the clock, I realized it was time for my pizza delivery. I'd almost forgotten about it. I walked up front with money in my hand. Just as I reached out to turn the deadbolt, the bell sounded again and again. Jeez, impatient much?

"Okay, okay, I'm coming. What do I owe?" As I glanced up, I realized Caleb was standing on the other side, not the pizza guy.

"Owe me what? I guess we'll have to discuss that," he said with a laugh.

I stepped back to let him inside and gave him a playful swat on the arm as he passed.

"What are you doing here?" I questioned.

"To see you, of course." He paused for a reaction. "Seriously, there was only so much of Janie's 'grieving' and drama I could take. Plus, I wanted to check in with you after last night's craziness. I know it was a lot to absorb."

He came to check on *me*? Interesting. Warmth blossomed in my chest. "Let's go back to my office. I was expecting the pizza delivery guy, but they must be running behind."

"Are you sure? I don't want to impose."

"Not at all. I was just looking over some files." Unsure if I wanted to tell him about my idea to investigate on my own, I played it cool as I led him down the hall.

Caleb smiled. "Okay, great!"

I hung my head. "Janie must be pretty devastated. I feel sick about it."

"I'm not so sure she's upset about losing Morgan so much as the loss of her feature that was going to run in the Ohio Bride Magazine."

"Wow. I don't blame you for wanting to get out of there."

When we reached my office, I waved him toward a chair.

"Have you heard any more from the police about your friend?" Caleb asked and took a seat.

"Not at all. Since she got arrested, they haven't been terribly forthcoming."

"I wish I could say I was shocked to hear that. I'm sorry."

"Thank you. Their suspicions couldn't be farther from the truth. Chelsea, a murderer? She doesn't have an evil bone in her body. I mean, yes, she may come off harsh sometimes, but under all that, she is a great friend, business partner and person," I explained.

"You're welcome," he replied.

I sat back in my chair and crossed my legs. "Have you found anything out yet?"

Caleb looked across at me and took a minute to answer. "To be honest, not much. As I mentioned, the former bride is an emotional mess. Mr. Coleman seems to be trying to do damage control with the media, and Mrs. Coleman has been more focused on not having an empty wineglass instead of consoling her daughter. I know Janie hired me, but there hasn't been a chance to speak to her alone. I haven't pressed it under the circumstances."

Hmm. He did come across as trustworthy and caring. Maybe I could tell him what I'd done so far. "That makes sense. After seeing Chelsea today and then learning The Wedded Bliss is getting sued, we've had a lot to deal with. Therefore, I have made an important decision."

"Oh?" Caleb asked, raising an eyebrow. "What is that?"

"I plan to find the real killer, and you're going to help me." I slapped the desk for emphasis.

His mouth dropped. "Wait, what? You own a wedding planning business, Leah. You don't know the first thing about investigation. Besides, it can be dangerous."

"I need to locate the killer before Chelsea is charged and sent up the river, so to speak. The victim was kind of a jerk, but no one deserves to be killed. Plus, it happened at my business. I refuse to let an evil person ruin my family's legacy."

"I know you want to help your friend, but why don't you just let the professionals do their job? I'm sure they can't think Chelsea really did this. She wasn't even there that night until she heard about it on the police scanner. I saw Morgan and his wounds. They were made by someone who had a real hatred for him. That person is dangerous."

"I appreciate your concern, but I need to do this. Are you in?"

Caleb's brow furrowed. "No matter what I say, and even if I don't help, you're going to do it anyway, aren't you?"

I nodded and smiled. "Yes, I am. If we work together, we'll be a great team. You have the experience as a private investigator while I have the determination and motivation."

He gave me a skeptical frown. "Are you sure?"

"Absolutely. Not only is Chelsea in jeopardy, but so is The Wedded Bliss. I can't afford to lose her or the business. It's the only thing I have left of my family."

"I understand that, but I could risk losing my license. You have to be willing to listen and take my advice. It's not going to be easy, and I cannot promise we'll solve this. I really want you to grasp what you're getting yourself into."

"I'm all in. I already started making some notes. If you'd like to scoot closer, I'll show you." When he'd complied, I slid my notepad across the desk. "I made a list of all the information I have about Janie and Morgan. I even checked local court records online and compiled a roster of people we need to interview."

Caleb skimmed through the pages. "Hmm, this is actually very impressive. It's a great start." He looked up at me. "I hope you realize you can count me out as a suspect?"

Oh, man, those eyes. His gaze got me all flustered. While I did want to agree with him, I still didn't know him that well. For all I knew, he could have killed Morgan and snuck back upstairs like nothing happened. For now, I was going to keep him on my list. I cleared my throat. "Of course, you were here when we found him missing. I was listing everyone."

"Is there anything you can remember about the crime scene that might be important?"

"Let me think." I replayed the gruesome moment in my head. "There was all the blood. Then I reached down to check his pulse. It was dark. Nothing appeared out of place, but the sword seemed very odd. I don't recall that we ever had swords," I commented.

"The watch! He was wearing a watch, and it was cracked," Caleb exclaimed as the memory hit him.

"Oh yes! I recall seeing that when I met with them to confirm the wedding details. It had a huge face and diamonds or crystals all around the edge which stuck out to me. I didn't think anything of it at that moment, except that it was very gaudy and flashy. Do you remember the specific time the watch showed?"

"Yes. Its hands were stopped at nine-seventeen."

Whew, the handsome investigator wasn't the killer after all. He arrived at my office at nine. "That was only about fifteen minutes before Adam arrived. What should we do now?" I asked.

"First, we'll need to speak to any of the guests, who were present, anyone who was close to Morgan, family, friends, etc. Most of them should still be at the hotel."

"We really need to talk to Theodore Banks. According to Mr. Coleman, he was the last person someone saw our victim talking to," I pointed out.

"I agree. Let's start with the groomsmen first. I'll call over to the Ashford Hotel," Caleb replied as he stepped out in the hall. A few minutes later, he came back in.

"Were you able to get hold of anyone?" I asked.

"Yes and no. I spoke with Logan and Evan but couldn't reach Cody."

"They were okay meeting with us?"

"Yes."

"We really need to learn more about him. Can you do a more extensive background check with your resources?"

"Of course. That will be the best place to start, but it may take time. You've already written down a lot to get us started. Now we need to delve a little deeper. May I use your laptop?" Caleb gestured towards my computer.

"Sure. Is it okay if I sit next to you?"

"Sure. The first thing I like to do is search court records. Most people don't realize how much these can tell you. Former addresses especially may help you find more acquaintances who may know your subject. One piece of the puzzle will lead to another, and so on and so forth." He continued to type.

He wasn't saying anything, but his brow was furrowed in deep concentration.

"Did you find anything?" I peered at the screen and tried to figure out what he was looking at.

"Not really, a speeding ticket here and there. I'll check for more when I get back to my room. I have some software programs on my computer I use. We'll go over tomorrow to the hotel and start talking to the groomsmen. Sound good?"

"Sure. What else can we do now?"

"Let's look at the rest of the suspect list. Janie, Mr. and Mrs. Coleman, the bridesmaids, Chelsea..."

"She is NOT a suspect," I grumbled.

"I know, calm down. We need to investigate everyone who was present, including the guests and your staff. Then we'll begin ruling them out."

"All right, I guess that makes sense."

Caleb and I had gotten off to a good start.

Before leaving for the day, Meg, Sally and I met. We decided to take a few days to re-group. Our customers were very understanding. As luck would have it, I only had to reschedule two events. My main goal going forward was to get Chelsea out of jail. She was my family and family sticks together. In all the years I had known her, she would never hurt a fly. She may have a gruff personality, but really was a teddy bear inside.

After we went our separate ways, I took a drive on some back roads, to give myself time to think and let everything percolate and . . . hopefully .

. . obtain more insight into the former groom to be. The most important interview right now would be with Ted Banks, the person who was last seen talking to Morgan.

CHAPTER SEVEN

I rose early the next morning and traveled downtown towards the courthouse annex. The town square was abuzz with activity. Lou's secretary called and let me know they set bail for Chelsea, and she could be released. My first stop was Carter's Bail Bonds, on Fern Street. It was the only one in Ashford. I lucked out and found an open parking meter in front of their office.

It wasn't much to look at. The white walls had become discolored with time and were covered in old nature scene paintings. A few ancient leather chairs with metal frames and a couple of wood end tables stacked with magazines populated the waiting area.

"Can I help you, honey?" A woman with one of the huskiest voices I'd ever heard approached the front desk. She'd teased and styled her bleach-blonde hair into an old-fashioned beehive. She was dressed in a short-sleeved striped blouse and tan slacks. She completed her look with blue eye shadow, round-framed glasses and bright red lipstick. An unlit cigarette hung from the corner of her mouth.

"Ahem, sorry. Yes, I need to bond out a friend," I responded.

"Their first and last name?" The cigarette bounced as she spoke.

"Chelsea Baker."

She looked over her glasses. "Her birthdate?"

"December eighth, 1987."

"I found her. Her bond was set at $10,000. We require ten percent down plus the one-hundred state fee. How would you like to pay for that?"

I plucked a card from my wallet and held it up. "Do you accept credit?"

"We take them all. The only things we can't are livestock and animals. We offer financing too," she replied.

"Could I put half on one card and the remainder on another?" I could already hear my bank account crying.

"Whatever works, sweetheart." The secretary tapped the clipboard. "Fill out this paperwork. I'll also need to make a copy of your license. Complete the lines that are highlighted. By signing these forms, you agree to all the terms and conditions. If the defendant fails to appear at their hearing, the amount of the bond is forfeited to the court and a warrant will be issued for the defendant's arrest," she rattled off.

I studied the papers and pointed to a particular section. "What about this?"

"Unfortunately, the state fee is non-refundable. Please fill out the indemnity agreement and a receipt."

"What happens next?" I asked.

"Once the paperwork is finalized and the payment has been processed, our bondsmen will post bail at the jail."

Jeez! I had no idea how involved this was. "How long does that take?"

"In most situations, we can process a bond within a few hours, then the individual will be released."

I filled everything out and made my payments. The clerk assured me they would contact me when it was paid so I could retrieve Chelsea. After I left the office, I headed back to The Wedded Bliss.

The woman from Carter's Bail Bonds contacted me a couple hours later to notify me that I could pick her up. I swung by Chelsea's place, fed Mr. Charlie, and selected a fresh set of clothes. On the way to the jail, I also stopped and picked up a coffee for each of us.

I gathered the bag I packed and entered the building. Sadly, Officer Smiley wasn't at the desk. A short, rotund older policeman with a grumpy face stood there instead.

"What do you need?" he grumbled.

"I am here to pick up Chelsea Baker, please," I responded.

"Have a seat, Miss. I'll call back and have them bring her up."

"Thank you."

I found a chair and waited. Ten minutes passed, then twenty, then thirty. Finally, the door opened, and an officer escorted her out to the front desk. She had to sign some paperwork, and they handed over her belongings. We ran towards each other and embraced. I stepped back and held her at arm's length to give her the once over. She didn't look any worse for wear.

"You're staring at me like you haven't seen me in weeks. It's been less than two days," Chelsea teased.

I shrugged. "I know, I know. Can't blame me for worrying."

"True. It wasn't as awful as you would think. Don't get me wrong. It wasn't great, but it wasn't terrible."

"I'm glad." I held up the bag I brought. "Thought you might want to change?"

Chelsea's face lit up. "Yes! Thank you! You're so thoughtful."

I gave her the clothes and shooed her away. "Go ahead. I'll wait, and then we can get out of here."

"Don't have to tell me twice." She walked down the hall to the public women's restroom.

Ten minutes later, she returned looking refreshed, and we left. When we reached my car and climbed inside, I handed her one of the coffees I bought and picked up my own.

"To freedom!" I crowed, tapping my cup against hers.

"Cheers!"

We made the drive to her place in companionable silence. I didn't want to bug her too much. I was sure she was exhausted physically and emotionally. We arrived at her apartment, and I made her promise to relax and check in with me later. I waited until she got inside before driving to the office.

The remainder of the workday flew by. Caleb called just before we closed and asked me to meet him in the parking lot of the Ashford Hotel. I located his gray pickup truck in the back. I pulled into a spot two down from him and met him at his driver's side door.

"About time you showed up, Jordan," he scolded as he stepped out.

I scoffed and smacked him gently on the shoulder. "I'm five minutes late. Give me a break."

He burst out laughing. "Just messing with you. Let's get going. Here's a small notebook and pen to take notes. Keep track of the room numbers and what you find out at each one. Once we finish the floor Morgan stayed on, we'll meet and come back here to discuss what we found."

"Got it. We need to know if there was anything they saw or heard the night of the bachelor party."

"Not bad. You're getting the hang of it."

We approached the lobby and took the elevator to the second floor. Caleb focused on one side of the hall, and I took the other.

I reached room 201 first and knocked but got no answer. The blare of a game show could be heard through the door. I tried again five seconds later, harder this time.

"What do you want?" a gravelly male voice called out.

"Sorry to bother you, sir. I wanted to ask you some questions about activities here at the hotel Thursday night," I explained. The door opened a crack and a bloodshot, blue eye peered out.

"Who are you?"

"My name is Leah Jordan. My associate and I are here to talk to people and see if they may have witnessed any incidents or noticed something out of the ordinary."

"The elephants? What elephants? This is a hotel!"

I raised my voice. "Incidents, I said in-ci-dents."

His shoulders dropped. "Oh, sorry, sweetheart. I can't hear so well these days. Don't get old. It's a pain in the ass," he groused.

I had to stifle a laugh. "I'll remember that. Sir, did you see anything Thursday night? A man who was staying here has been murdered," I explained.

He rubbed his chin. "You mean the young guns who were here? Can't say that I did. Oh, wait. One of those dancing girls knocked on my door, but I didn't answer it. I kept an eye on her through the peephole. She was a fine-looking woman."

I inwardly groaned. "Is there anything else you can tell me?"

"No. I need to get back to my program now. Alex Trebek is on, and I never miss an episode."

"Of course. Thank you for your time."

Before I could finish my sentence, he slammed the door.

I continued down the hall to question any other guests who might be available. Most of them had no answers, and one lady had just checked in earlier in the day. It wasn't until I reached the room next to where Morgan and his groomsmen stayed that I found another witness. A young woman scantily clad in a hot pink crop top and tight jeans came to the door. Her rainbow bob swung just above her shoulders, and a huge sparkling diamond stud decorated her nose. I figured it had to be fake.

Her furrowed brow and frown expressed her displeasure. "What?"

"Sorry to bother you. I was just wondering if you were here Thursday night and witnessed anything?"

She rolled her eyes. "I already told the police what I know."

"I understand that, ma'am, but it would really help if you could disclose to me what you shared with them."

She let out the longest sigh. "My girlfriends and I went out to dinner and a club in the city. I met a hottie, and we came back here. One thing led to another, and you know..." she said, her voice trailing off while she winked.

"Did you hear anything when you returned? See anyone suspicious in the hallway?"

She crossed her arms and tapped her feet. "I heard what sounded like a fight but didn't think much of it."

I waited for her to elaborate, but she didn't. My patience started to wear thin. "Were you able to make out what was being said?"

She shook her head. "I told you. I was a little busy. It was pretty muffled anyway.

This was like pulling teeth. "Did you look out or open the door?"

She uncrossed her arms, and her right hand reached up to fiddle with an earring. "My date got up and looked through the peephole but couldn't see anything. Then the noise stopped, and he came back to bed. That was it."

"Could I have the name of your companion? I'd like to talk to him as well."

"I don't remember. Jason, Jackson, maybe it was Jonathan."

Of course. "Thank you. You've been a great help. Here's my number if you think of anything else."

She took the card from my hand and shut the door.

I returned to the end of the hallway and met with Caleb. "All done?"

"Just finished up. Let's head somewhere we can talk and compare notes," he suggested.

"Sounds great."

We left the hotel and agreed to meet back at my office. I beat him there and got settled at my desk. He showed up two minutes later.

He plopped down in a chair across from me. "How did you do?"

"I struck out for the most part, but there were a couple of people who had some information. You?"

"The majority of the individuals on my side didn't check into the hotel until after Saturday. However, one person I spoke with mentioned something interesting."

"Oh yeah?"

He opened his notebook and glanced at a page. "The guy's name was Mark Brown. He traveled to town for a business conference at the Columbus Convention Center. He and a few other colleagues went out later that evening and returned to the hotel around two in the morning. He stated when they got back, they overheard people arguing."

"I also had one of the guests report she heard something similar. Did your witness make out anything specific?"

"He only mentioned hearing pieces and parts. A couple of words he could understand were 'money' and 'threat'."

"Money and threat. We'll have to figure out how that may connect to Morgan," I murmured.

"Did you discover any information?"

"The old man in room 206 told me about a stripper who came to his door. The girl was looking for the party she was supposed to work that evening."

"He sent her away. What a gentleman." Caleb chuckled.

"Trust me. It was all I could do not to laugh. He was in his boxers and undershirt." As soon as I recalled that image, I shivered.

"Were you able to find out anything else?"

"The only other information I received was that they were loud and obnoxious. After some of the guests called the front desk a gazillion times, things calmed down."

He closed his notepad. "Now we need to determine who was involved. After we interview the groomsmen, I hope that the pieces will come together."

"Let's call it a night. I'm beat, and I'm sure you are as well."

"Sounds good," he agreed. "I may work some more when I get to my room. Check and see if any new information came in. We'll meet up in the morning so we can begin the interviews."

"Perfect. I'll just let Sally know in case she needs anything."

CHAPTER EIGHT

The next morning, I woke up to a text from Caleb asking me to meet him at Maisie's Café in an hour. I grabbed a quick shower and went to pick out a nice but comfortable outfit. After a quick shower and a few moments of indecision, I opted for a nice yet comfortable pair of khakis, a short-sleeved, green and white dressy top, and brown flats.

I pulled my hair up in a ponytail and took care of the cats before I left. The café was in Uptown Ashford, close to the residence of the first person we planned to interview, Janie Coleman. The investigator laid on the charm to convince her to meet him.

The smell of freshly brewed coffee wafted into my nostrils when I walked inside. I spotted Caleb sitting at a little table, just past the front counter. He held up two mugs and called me over. Perfect, he'd already ordered.

As I approached, he stood up and pulled out the chair across from his.

"Good morning, thank you." I sat down.

He looked handsome today in a dark green shirt which complimented his eyes. I caught a whiff of soap and sandalwood mixed with hints of citrus. I began to picture him in the shower, soap suds running down his muscled chest as beads of water fell down his body. My cheeks grew warm. I glanced over and caught Caleb staring at me.

His face bore a look of concern. "Jordan? Are you okay? Why's your face red?"

My hands flew up to my face. I did feel a little warm. Oh my gosh Leah, focus! Now is not the time! I grabbed my coffee and took a sip. "I'm fine, not sure what it could be. How are you doing?"

His eyebrows raised as if he didn't believe me, but he didn't question it any further. "Not bad. Are you prepared to talk to Janie?"

I plucked my notebook from my bag and placed it on the table. "As ready as I'll ever be. What's the plan?"

"I figure we'll just keep it straightforward. Gather more background information on her and Morgan and their relationship. Then see where it takes us," he replied.

"Sounds good." I took a sip of my coffee. "Maybe she'll shed some light on anyone else who has had an issue with her fiancé."

"Exactly. The more details we can learn, the more suspects we may uncover."

I stood up and slung my bag on my shoulder. "Did you want to take one car?"

Caleb nodded as he pushed his chair in. "Yes, if that's okay. There isn't any reason to take two."

"I'm ready if you are," I commented.

"Let's head out," he agreed.

"Janie, I appreciate you meeting with us. I realize it's not under ideal circumstances, but we really want to find out who did this," Caleb explained.

The socialite, in a light blue maxi dress and strappy silver heels, perched on an ornate pink high-backed chair. Her right foot bounced, and she looked like she'd just gnawed on a lemon. This was going to be a fun interview.

"I don't understand why you're here. I told the police everything I knew. Morgan was speaking with Theodore, and then he was murdered," she huffed, crossing her arms and slouching in her seat. "Shouldn't you be talking to him? I'll double what I was paying you if you solve this before they do. What am I going to say to people? How can I even show my face at the club now? Everyone will be pointing and whispering, 'There she goes, the woman whose fiancé was killed'." Tears ran down her cheeks and she started to sniffle.

Oh jeez. It seemed like she was more concerned about her reputation than getting justice. I pulled a pack of tissues from my bag and offered them to her. "Here. You, don't want your mascara to run."

She plucked one out and dabbed at her eyes. She mumbled something that may have resembled appreciation.

"While I understand your frustration, this conversation is just as important because it could provide us with information that could lead to a suspect," my colleague reasoned.

"Fine. What do you want to know?" she sighed.

You would think we were ruining her day when all we wanted to do was help her find out who killed her fiancé.

"Let's start from the beginning. How did you and Morgan meet?" I asked.

A dreamy look fell over her face. "It was about two years ago, and I went to visit Daddy at the office for our weekly lunch. I was late and ran across the lobby to catch the elevator. My new Manolos weren't broken in yet, and I tripped. He caught me and the rest is history. We began seeing each other at dinners, social events in Columbus, the orchestra—it was a whirlwind."

Caleb looked up from his notes. "Did you know your fiancé worked at Coleman Industries?"

"Not at first. He ended up telling me later," Janie explained.

Why wouldn't he be upfront with that information, unless he was hiding something? I tucked that thought away for later. "How did your father feel about it?"

She shrugged. "Daddy was a little peeved initially, but he got over it. I'm his princess. He could never stay mad at me. If I'm happy, he's happy."

Caleb continued. "How did they get along?"

"Fine. He started taking him golfing and to the country club. He doesn't take just anyone," she responded.

"How would you describe your relationship with your fiancé?" I asked.

"We were the perfect couple, of course. My darling spoiled me, and treated me to spa days and fancy dinners. A true gentleman..." She sighed wistfully and got a faraway look in her eyes as if replaying those moments in her head.

"Janie, no one is without flaws. There weren't any bad habits, things that annoyed you, drove you mad that he did?" Caleb pressed.

"Hmm, let me think." She paused for a moment before shaking her head. "Not really. Although he was a workaholic. But as Daddy explained, that only meant he would be a good provider."

I doubted that logic. "Anything else you noticed?"

"I guess there was the fact he was always on his phone. Texting, calls, emails, every day. Sometimes I would have to plead with him to stop all that nonsense and pay attention to me."

Jeez, if Janie was my girlfriend, I didn't blame the guy.

He scribbled on his notepad. "You two were getting married. How was the planning going?"

Tears formed again in the corners of her eyes. She pulled out another tissue and wiped them away. "It was lovely until this. Daddy let me have whatever I wanted. My fiancé let me make all the important decisions on the colors, the theme, et cetera," she answered, still dabbing.

"Ms. Coleman, I understand this is difficult. These questions will help uncover what happened to your fiancé. Did he have any enemies?" he asked.

"Not at all. He was liked by everyone. There was this particular instance, but I'm not sure. No one comes to mind. There was this particular instance, but I'm not sure," she hesitated.

"Could you elaborate?" I inquired.

"A few weeks ago, we were preparing for a charity benefit, and Morgan had to leave the bedroom abruptly. I assumed maybe he had left something downstairs. When I tried to ask him what was going on, he stepped out onto the balcony and made a call. Once he turned to face away from me, I inched closer to him. He was talking pretty softly at first. Then his voice grew louder with a hint of frustration or anger," she explained.

"Could you make out what he said?" Caleb asked.

"Not really. I did catch, '...the money better be paid or else'," her voice trailed off.

The hairs on my arms stood up. "Are you positive about what you heard?"

She nodded. "I wrote it off as some kind of business call or related to our weekend. Morgan was planning a huge surprise for us, but he wouldn't spill. The silly man."

Caleb glanced up from his notes. "Can you think of *anything* further that we should know?"

"Not really." She gave an impatient flounce. "Are we done here? I'm late for my spa appointment," she whined.

If I was a different person, I would have reached over and slapped her. Who could be so concerned with pampering after some villain just murdered her fiancé?

"For now. We may have more follow-up questions later. We'll be in touch, and we appreciate your time," my partner concluded.

"I hope you find them. Thank you for coming. Hilda can show you out." Janie left the room and a couple minutes later the maid returned.

"Have a good afternoon," she said, holding the door open as we passed by.

"Thanks," we responded in unison.

He drove me back to the cafe so I could pick up my car, and we met at my office to go over what we'd learned.

"What do you think about Janie?" I asked as we carried our coffee mugs to the conference room table.

He raised an eyebrow at me. "That she's the most self-absorbed person to roam this earth?"

"And ruin her standing in society? No. She is all about getting into the best social circles and becoming a trophy wife. Plus, I don't think she'd want to chip a nail," he responded seriously.

We both looked at each other and burst out laughing.

"May not be very appropriate to be joking about it," I tried to say with a straight face, picturing Janie having a cow over a ruined manicure.

Caleb cleared his throat. "No, probably not. Unless the spoiled rich girl persona is a very well put together act, I think we can rule her out."

"I agree. Only a few gazillion more people to go," I sighed.

"We need to retrace our victim's last steps in the days leading up to the rehearsal."

"Janie provided us with a copy of their wedding weekend itinerary. We set up a spa day for the ladies and the men played a round of golf that morning. Then they planned a lunch so the bride and groom could go to their respective bachelor and bachelorette parties later that evening." I took the folder from my bag and flipped through it until I found the schedule. "Here it is." I handed it over to Caleb.

"You were there. Do you remember seeing anything or anyone strange or odd that day?"

"I was so busy running around, making sure things went off without a hitch, I didn't have a chance to notice. Janie was a real stickler about everything staying on time," I explained.

"Where did Morgan and his groomsmen go?"

I pointed. "According to this sheet, they went to Columbus to explore the bars in the Short North, ending at the Ashford Hotel that evening while the girls went to Miss Hilary's Tea Room."

"Let's divide and conquer. I'll visit the bars, and you check out the tearoom."

My eyebrows raised. "Oh, I get the tearoom because I'm the girl? No way, Jose. We're sticking together."

"Has anyone told you lately that you are one of the most stubborn women?" he growled, trying to suppress a grin.

I smiled and shrugged my shoulders. "I may be, but I have a lot at stake. I want to make sure we find the real killer. Maybe it's the curious person in me, but I am interested in knowing everything that's happening."

Caleb cocked his head and teased, "It appears like you don't trust me."

I gasped in mock horror. "I wouldn't say that at all!"

He looked at me and raised his eyebrows. "Fine. Be ready to think on your feet and pretend at a moment's notice if you need to. Can you handle that?"

"Think, pretend. Got it." I gave him a thumbs up.

"We'll want to start with the patrons and the staff. I'll pull the car around. Be ready in five."

I quickly applied some lip gloss. Once outside, I slid into the front passenger seat of his SUV, and we took off. He decided we would make our way to the hotel tavern first, have a couple of drinks, and see if we could engage anyone in conversation. After we arrived, we snatched two stools at the bar.

"Good evening. My name is Max. What can I get you?" the bartender asked as he approached us.

His awful black goatee needed a trim and didn't match his short blonde hair. When he set a couple of little white bar napkins down in front of us, I had to look away so I wouldn't stare at his abnormally large muscles fighting to escape his very tight shirt.

Caleb peered at the row of taps behind the bar. "I'll have that Irish red you have on draft, and my lady will have an amaretto sour."

He turned away to make our drinks.

I nudged my companion in the side. "I can order for myself."

"I know, Jordan, but we're supposed to be a couple, remember?" he whispered.

A few minutes later, Max returned with our beverages.

"It's pretty about awful what happened the other night, wasn't it?" Caleb mused.

The bartender murmured. "Such a shame. Nice young man."

"Did you know him?" I interjected.

He poured a couple of beers for one of the waitresses. "Not really. He and his buddies had quite a few. Bachelor party, I reckon it was. The group was a little rowdy but not too out of control."

"I heard the police think it was a result of an altercation at the bar," my partner commented.

Max glanced up at us. "Where'd you hear that?"

"I can't remember," Caleb replied.

He finished pouring the last beer and gave us a stare. "You two sure have a lot of questions. Are you reporters?"

I shook my head. "No, we're not."

"I'm Caleb, a private investigator, and this is my associate, Leah. We've been hired by the family to investigate the case.

He shrugged. "Figured you were something. Not the usual bar patrons we're used to."

Was that a compliment or an insult? I wasn't sure. I swirled my straw in my drink, making the cherry dance in my glass.

"Were there any altercations the other night?" Caleb questioned.

Max sighed. "We already told the cops what we know. Why don't you ask them?"

"Look, we're not trying to cause an issue. We owe it to the family to find out what happened. We'd really appreciate you talking to us, too."

"All right, I get what you're saying. The other night, the wife of one of our regulars, Diane, was here with some of her girlfriends. It was eighties themed, and the girls were drunk and making fools of themselves on the dance floor. She started dancing with a guy from the bachelor party. Diane's husband walked in, and she was caught red-handed. The next thing I knew, there was a big commotion, and she was pretending to be offended and disgusted by the dude she was humping all over two seconds before. She ended up breaking a beer bottle over the poor guy's head."

"Whoa, that's a little drastic," I piped up.

"Was he doing something inappropriate? Do you recall which male it was? Was it the one who was just found murdered?" Caleb asked.

His brow furrowed as he tried to remember. "Not that I could tell. In all the chaos, I can't say for sure. The other party members came rushing over to try to get their friend off the dance floor once she started freaking out."

Dang! She hit him on the head. I thought back to the night of the rehearsal dinner when I saw Morgan and Janie. I didn't recall noticing any sign of an injury, but of course, I wasn't looking for one either at the time. "Was he okay?"

"Yup. I guess she didn't want her old man to know she was hitting on somebody else…" The bartender trailed off as he got called away by a patron at the other end of the bar.

"We should talk to Diane's husband," he suggested.

"You think that's a good idea?" I wondered.

"Male testosterone plus jealousy and alcohol is a bad combination. It's an angle we should check out. While Max says he didn't see who was hit. Who knows what occurred after Morgan and his bachelor party left? Husbands usually don't take too kindly to someone messing with their wives." He signaled the bartender so we could pay our bill.

When he returned, he pointed to our glasses. "You two need another round?"

"Thanks, but I think we're good. We want to close our tab," Caleb replied.

He nodded. "You got it. I'll be right back."

"One more thing. Do you mind giving me the name of Diane's husband?" inquired the private investigator. "I just have a few questions we'd like to ask him."

"Deaver. Marcus Deaver," Max responded.

"Thanks, we appreciate it." Caleb pulled out his wallet, plucked out two twenty-dollar bills, and placed them on the bar.

The bartender returned from helping another guest and saw the money. "Oh, that's too much."

"Keep it."

We left and returned to the car.

"It was actually better, and more fruitful than I thought," I remarked.

"Right. We know Morgan and his group were here, and there was an altercation involving a bar patron. Whether Marcus Deaver decided to retaliate and acted, is yet to be determined."

"Now, to check out the rest of the bars."

The drive to the Short North was uneventful. We found a public parking garage and walked from bar to bar. Most people thought our victim looked familiar but couldn't recall anything specifically related to the night they were there. We passed out several of Caleb's business cards in case anyone remembered him or his friends. The tearoom was a bust too. After the long exhausting day, he took me back to my office, and we decided to meet up the following day.

Another all the investigating, I was ready to get in my pajamas and veg out. Hopefully, the cats would agree. I clutched my purse and the bag from Alvin's Deli and walked towards the house.

Once I approached the front porch, I noticed a small blue box tied shut with a white ribbon partially covered by the mat. A delivery? I wasn't expecting anything. I scooped it up. Patches and Oreo ran from the back hallway, voicing their enthusiasm at my return.

"Why hello you two. Let me guess, you're hungry? I placed my bags on the table in the hall and made my way into the kitchen to fill their food bowls. They normally had supersonic hearing and would come running by the time the first kibble hit the bowl, no matter their location in the house. I set them down but noticed the girls hadn't followed me. Weird.

"Guys, come and get it!" I called, as I went back to the front hall. Both of them, with their hair sticking straight up, surrounded the blue box, which was now on the floor. Oreo took her right paw and swiped at it.

"Girls, that's not yours. Stop or you'll rip it up. Let me look. Maybe it's catnip." I couldn't figure out why they were acting so strangely.

I picked it up and brought it into the kitchen by the sink. I shook it a little. There was *definitely* something inside. I untied the ribbon and lifted the lid.

I screamed.

"Oh my god! What the heck?"

Inside, on top of some white tissue, lay the body of a very dead bird. Attached to its left leg was a small note. Gross. I didn't want to touch it, but my curiosity got the best of me. Who would send me this?

Grimacing with disgust, I untied the string holding the message on the tiny corpse and carefully unrolled it with my fingernails, trying to handle it as little as possible. In bold print type was the message: 'Drop it, or you're next'. Shaking, I dropped the bird inside the box and slammed the lid shut. Someone knew I was looking into Morgan's death and apparently didn't like it. I had to tell someone, but I refrained from calling the police or worrying Meg and Chelsea. Who did that leave? Caleb.

I pushed the offensive package further away from me on the counter and frantically washed my hands, hoping I didn't get any dead bird cooties on me. The girls were eating, so I went to the living room and dialed Caleb's number. Three rings, no answer. I was about to hang up when his deep, sexy voice came over the line.

"Leah? What's up?"

Butterflies tickled my stomach. "Oh, nothing much. Relaxing, fed the cats, received a lifeless bird in a box, going to catch up on some TV shows. What about you?"

"Whoa, back up. Did you say someone left you a dead bird?" he exclaimed. I could tell the gears were turning in his head.

"Um...yep. Dead as a door nail," I confirmed.

"No return address?"

"Nope, none. It did have a nice little threatening note tied around one of the bird's legs."

His voice deepened. "What kind of threat?"

Aww! Was that concern I heard in his tone? The way he spoke made me think he was about to go beat someone up for sending me the warning.

"They want me to stop investigating."

"I'll be over." *Click.*

He wasn't kidding. Ten minutes later, he knocked on my door.

He wasted no time. As soon as I let him in, he demanded, "Where is it? Show it to me."

"It's in the kitchen on the counter." I pointed down the hall.

He took off, and I followed behind.

Caleb picked the box up and turned it over. "This is it? There was no outside packaging or a return address?"

I shook my head. "Nothing. There was a ribbon. The white one lying there to the left. Who would do this?"

"A coward," he growled as he placed it back on the counter.

"Should we call the police?"

His expression grew serious as he fixed me with his gorgeous green-eyed gaze. "Leah, look, I don't think you should investigate anymore."

My jaw dropped. "Excuse me? I'm not going to sit back and twiddle my thumbs while I hope the killer's caught."

"They'll catch them but if your life is in danger, it's time to withdraw. Let the professionals handle it."

Professionals? Hmph! I would show him! I'd figure out who killed Morgan and restore The Wedded Bliss's reputation, with or without Caleb. "Fine," I grumbled.

"Oh, don't be like that. It's for your safety!" he exclaimed, running his hands through his hair.

"You just think I'm some fluffy-headed girl who runs a wedding business, but you are mistaken." My face grew warm in proportion to my mounting frustration.

The attraction I harbored for him warred with a terrible feeling of betrayal. How did he dare assume I was incapable of taking care of myself? Was I useless to him this whole time? Did he have me along just for company without thinking I'd be able to make a valid contribution? Steam may have puffed out of my ears if his expression was any indication.

He held his hands out as if trying to calm a crazy person. "Now you're putting words in my mouth."

"It's time you left. I called you for help, to figure out what we need to do next, not to get told to butt out. I'm done talking about it." My hand shot out to point at the door.

I noticed he flinched, much to my satisfaction.

"Leah, come on, we're a team..."

"And take the bird with you." I picked up the box and shoved it into his hands.

He looked like he was going to say something else, thought better of it, and bowed his head as he walked toward the front. He glanced back once when he reached the porch. I slammed the door, still disgusted by the package and filled with guilt about fighting with Caleb.

CHAPTER NINE

The fight with Caleb still bothered me the next day. I overreacted. I knew the dead bird concerned him, but my parents raised me to take care of myself. We were already so far into the investigation. We couldn't turn back now. I hoped calling him and clearing the air could get us re-focused.

My nerves jangled as I dialed. When he answered on the second ring, my stomach seized up.

I had to focus to keep my voice steady. "Morning. Do you have a few minutes to talk?"

"Are you sure you reached the right number? You were fast to get rid of me yesterday," he remarked.

"I'm sorry. I was freaked out, and I may have overreacted," I babbled. "I have been under a lot of stress since I took over at The Wedded Bliss. Plus, it's not every day you receive a dead bird as a gift...er, threat."

"Jordan, it's all right. I'm sorry for getting so frustrated, but I won't apologize for the concern. This person has killed once. He'll do it again."

Jordan? Was that sweet, or did he consider me just one of the guys? I shook my head. Such trivialities weren't important right now. "Can we just move on? We do make a good team, and there is a lot more ground to cover."

"I agree. I've been doing a little footwork. After we left the bar the other night, I conducted some computer searches and located an address and phone number for Marcus Deaver. He's willing to speak with us," Caleb told me.

"Really? That's great!" I exclaimed.

"We're meeting him this afternoon down at the Ashford Tavern. Can you be there at 5 p.m.?"

"Sounds good. I'll see you then."

I arrived at the restaurant, surprised to find it wasn't packed for a Wednesday night. Known for their happy hour, it was the place to come after work to unwind with co-workers and have a few drinks. Blue collar, white collar, they catered to everyone. I located Caleb on the right and found him at a table covered by food.

He waved his hand over the spread and smiled. "Hope you don't mind. I was starving. Picked out a few different appetizers to share."

"Not at all, thanks," I replied as I plucked a mozzarella stick from one of the platters. "We need to find out what Mr. Deaver remembers about that night."

"Exactly. While also determining if the incident at the bar continued outside after they all left and that's who our witness overheard arguing in the hotel later. If he decided to follow Morgan and his friends and retaliate, we may have found our suspect."

"Or he could not even be connected at all. Do you really think he would agree to meet with us if he was a killer, though? He'd hardly admit to anything that could get him charged or sued."

"You would be surprised. Some criminals get off by placing themselves in the middle of the investigation. I told him we were with an insurance company, following up on a claim made by the bar regarding a possible incident. I didn't say anything about his involvement."

I nibbled on a tortilla chip I filled with spinach artichoke dip. "Smart."

Caleb smoothed down his shirt and ran his fingers through his hair. "You take notes. I'll ask the questions. I've done a few of these types of interviews previously."

"I can do that. I'll move some of this food out of the way so it's not a distraction."

We did not have to wait much longer for Mr. Deaver to arrive. I wasn't sure what I expected as he approached our table, but it wasn't someone so handsome. He wore a nice gray polo shirt, khaki pants, and black loafers, and seemed to be in his mid to late forties. Who would want to cheat on him? Caleb and I both rose to greet him.

"Good afternoon, Mr. Deaver. My name is Caleb Hamilton, we spoke on the phone. Please have a seat."

"Thank you."

He gave a curt nod and took a chair across from us.

I pulled out my notebook and turned to a blank page.

Caleb began the interview. "Let me introduce my associate, Leah Jordan. She will be taking notes. First, can you state your full name and address?"

"Marcus Allen Deaver. 3467 Pinecrest Drive, Ashford Ohio."

"On the night of Thursday, June 17th, 2014, were you present at the Ashford Hotel bar?"

He nodded. "Yes, I was."

His cooperation thus far gave me a little trickle of relief. I hoped it would continue.

My partner looked at him directly. "Sir, what was your purpose for being there?"

"I was meeting my wife for drinks after work."

"Did you witness an altercation that evening?"

His eyes narrowed, and his demeanor changed a bit. "What does this have to do with an insurance claim? I thought you said there was an accident that night and someone was suing the restaurant?"

"Sir, we're just trying to figure out the whole picture of the events. Per the information we've received, the altercation involved a few people, including you and your wife. There were also reports of damage." Caleb tried to put him at ease while maintaining his momentum with the interview.

Mr. Deaver settled back in his chair again. "Yes, something happened, but it was all a big misunderstanding."

"Could you be more specific?"

"A guy was hitting on my wife. When she wasn't receptive to his advances, he tried to get rough with her, and she defended herself."

"What did you do?"

"I stepped in and pulled her away from him. Made sure she was okay and not hurt, then we left."

"Nothing further was said or happened between you and him?"

"No, sir. He was obviously wasted. His buddies came over, apologized and they took their friend and exited the bar."

"You didn't want to get him back for messing with your wife? Did you follow them outside after you left?"

"No, I'm not that kind of person. Everyone was looking at us, and it'd been a long day. I just wanted to take her and go home."

I didn't blame him. It would have embarrassed me, too.

"Did you see any destruction to the bar?" Caleb asked.

"I don't remember," Marcus Deaver responded, though he had regained his initial calm attitude.

"Can anyone vouch for you and your wife after you went home?"

He nodded. "Our babysitter, Sarah. My wife hired her to watch the kids. After we returned, she left."

Caleb cocked his head. "What time would you say that the two of you arrived back at your residence?"

"Around 10:30 p.m. We only had the sitter till 11 p.m."

I made sure to put a star by the time frame in my notes. Need to verify that.

"Would you mind giving me Sarah's contact information, so I am able to follow up with her?"

He shrugged. "I can get it from my wife and call you tomorrow. Is there anything else you need to know?"

"I think we're good. This concludes our interview. Thank you for meeting with us." He handed Mr. Deaver his business card as the men rose and shook hands.

It had been a few days since we received the lawsuit notice at my business. I thought I should meet with Lou again for an update and to figure out what to do next.

I entered his office and approached the front desk.

"Good afternoon! Lou's just finishing up with a client on the phone and then he'll call you back. Make yourself comfortable. Can I fetch you a coffee or water?" Patty asked.

"Thanks, I'm fine."

I took a seat in the lobby. No matter what happened, we would get through this. I kept repeating it over and over in my head. I picked up one of the magazines off the coffee table and had just started flipping through it when Lou came out.

"Leah, nice to see you again." His friendly greeting gave me a hint of hope. "Let us go back to my office."

Once we were settled, he pulled out a folder that contained the documents I'd been served. He said nothing or several seconds. The silence was deafening. I wasn't sure if it was a good or bad sign that he hadn't spoken yet.

"Now you've had time to investigate things, give it to me straight. Do you think they have a case?" I posed the question.

He sat back in his chair and rested his hands on his stomach. "On the surface, no, I don't. It appears the Colemans are upset and looking for someone to blame. They are suing for emotional suffering and damages."

Wow, unbelievable!

"What should we do?" Annoyed, I wondered in the back of my mind if we could file a counterclaim for the same thing.

"I'll begin developing a defense in the meantime, just in the event we need it. For now, it's best if you continue with business as usual. I'm still working to get the charges against Chelsea dismissed. Once that happens and the police find the real perpetrator, I feel the suit will be dropped, too."

"I hope so," I responded.

"I need to prepare for my next meeting, but I'll keep you in the loop. Don't comment or answer any questions about it. Direct any inquiries to my office," he instructed.

I rose to leave. "Got it. Thanks again, Lou."

"Anything for you, my dear," he smiled.

chapter ten

Caleb and I planned to meet at the Ashford Hotel before we interviewed the groomsmen. I wanted to look professional but also keep the guys' attention. I opted to stray from my usual attire and selected a nice turquoise low-cut shirt, a short black skirt, and silver sandals. Normally I would have a sweater on top, but if it greased the wheels a little, I was willing to buck tradition.

There were hardly any cars in the lot when I arrived. I strolled in and took a seat in the lobby while I waited for him. To pass the time, I decided to look through the notes we had made before.

Before I finished reviewing them, Caleb showed up with a cup of coffee for me. It smelled divine. A quick glance told me he was definitely worth waiting on. The light jacket he wore did little to hide his tight black T-shirt that emphasized his chest muscles. My eyes continued downward to take in his well-fitting pair of blue jeans and scuffed brown cowboy boots.

Focus, Leah! "Oh, uh, thank you," I stammered before taking a sip.

"Morning, Jordan. No second thoughts?" he asked, as he sat next to me.

"Nope. I told you I'm all in, and I meant that. Who are we interviewing first?"

"We'll be talking to Logan. I've already called up to his room, so he should be down shortly. I set up separate appointments for each grooms-man with some time in between."

"Sounds great. Now remind me how Morgan knew him." I set my coffee down and picked up my notebook and pen to jot down his name.

"He's a friend from college. He and our victim couldn't be any tighter. Wherever one went, the other was not too far behind, I've learned."

I created a column under Logan and wrote as I remarked, "They've remained close I assume, since he was asked to be a groomsman."

"Exactly. Hence why I felt he should be the first person we talked with."

"Smart idea, Mr. Hamilton," I said with a wink.

Caleb laughed. "Let's set some goals we want to accomplish. If we have a plan of action, it increases our chances of finding out information that can help us clear Chelsea and locate the real killer."

"We need to determine their alibis, their relationships with our victim, if they had any issues with him, stuff like that, right?" I rattled off.

He raised an eyebrow. "Exactly. You're getting pretty good at investigating."

I smiled. "Don't look so surprised. I've watched a lot of crime shows. There's more to me than weddings, flowers and cakes."

"I'm discovering that," he chuckled.

"Who's going to lead the questioning?"

"Why not let me start, and you can interject if you think of something?" Also, would you mind taking notes?"

"Not a problem." I held up my pen. "I've already started."

"Here he comes." Caleb stood up to greet him and shake hands.

I jumped up too fast and whacked my leg on the coffee table. Ignoring the sharp pain that shot through my limb, I clenched my jaw and tried to pretend nothing had happened.

Logan possessed average country club boy good looks with short blonde hair and blue eyes. His slender five-nine frame was dressed in a hunter green polo shirt and khakis.

How long was my knee going to throb? I forced a smile and stuck my right hand out toward him. "Glad you could meet with us."

He shook it and chose a chair across from us. "Sure. What's going on?"

Caleb started. "As a result of recent events, I'm investigating Morgan's murder."

The confusion was evident on his face. "I thought the police were already handling that."

"They are, but I have been hired to look into it as well," my partner explained.

He sat up straighter and cleared his throat. "How can I help?"

"You were both very close. How did Morgan act in the days leading up to the rehearsal dinner?"

"Like he always did. Working a ton, stressed and nervous. What man wouldn't be? This would be the end of his bachelorhood." the groomsman joked.

"True. Did he appear to be having any issues with anyone?" Caleb inquired.

"Not really. Morgan was a shrewd businessman, but he was a great person under the tough exterior. I knew he had some big project he was spending a lot of time on," Logan responded.

"Do you know what kind?"

He shook his head. "No, he never discussed work in detail. Just the typical stuff, sports, the news, stocks, etc."

"I understand this has been challenging for you and emotions are still raw, but if there is anything you can recollect, please reach out. Regardless of whether it seems minor, or even trivial, it could be important."

"I will. Thank you for looking into this," he replied.

We stood up and shook hands again. Caleb handed Logan one of his business cards before he walked away towards the elevators.

"That wasn't much help," I commented.

"Now, you never know. He might think of something and contact us. Be patient, grasshopper," he chuckled.

I liked to think I had a few good virtues, but patience was not one of them. "Me? You are funny. How can I?"

"I just meant that it takes time to find the answers we are seeking. Let's gear up for the next interview." Caleb pulled out a list from his pocket. "Cody Hayes was the only one of Morgan's groomsmen who was also a co-worker."

"Maybe we'll be able to gain some insight into the big project he was working on, which may give us new information we can explore."

"Exactly. At least we hope so."

Ten minutes later, he walked into the lobby. Tall, handsome, and fit, he'd plastered a pleasant smile on his friendly face as he approached.

We greeted him and settled back down at the table.

"We appreciate you meeting with us. We're here to discuss what occurred at the rehearsal dinner."

"Not entirely sure how much help I can offer," Cody shrugged.

"Every little detail could be of importance. We all want to see justice for Morgan," I urged.

My words seemed to have resonated.

His shoulders relaxed. "Yes, of course."

Caleb opened with, "Did you notice anything strange with him in the days leading up to the rehearsal dinner?"

"Not really. He's a guy who works better under pressure. We were trying to land a huge client, and we'd done nothing but eat and breathe this project. Although now that I think about it, he did seem more stressed than usual. I stopped by his office one day and found him murmuring to himself while staring at his cell phone. When I asked him if everything was okay, he got short with me, and said he was fine," Cody responded.

That tracked with what the bride had told us previously.

"When was the last time you saw Morgan that evening?" Caleb asked.

"We were having a few cocktails at the cash bar. Janie gets all bitchy if he indulges too much, but it was a celebration, so why the heck not?"

"How many would you say he'd had?"

Cody shrugged. "Some shots with all of us, maybe a few mixed drinks."

I glanced up from my notes. "Did he appear happy? Upset? Nervous?"

"A little anxious perhaps, but nothing he couldn't manage."

Caleb stuck with job related questions. "Besides the big client, were there any issues at work?"

"The usual office politics. We worked in teams and there was always rivalry between them. Mr. Coleman focused on results. He wanted to go international with the company which led to a contest. Nobody wants to disappoint Coleman," Cody explained.

"Which team was your biggest competition?"

The groomsman thought for a minute before he answered. "I guess it would be Theodore Banks. He was an old friend of Coleman's, and everyone already thinks he receives preferential treatment."

I made a notation on the page and drew a huge star by his name. "Did they ever get into any altercations?" I asked.

"Sure. It was a high-stress situation. Especially during crunch time. It always felt like he was trying to top Morgan."

Interesting. Some professional jealousy existed. Could that have been enough to lead to murder? "How so?"

"Once, Ted stole one of his potential clients right out from under him."

Caleb sat up in his chair. "What did Morgan do?"

"He tried to bring it to Mr. Coleman's attention, but when they confronted him, Ted said it was a misunderstanding, and nothing more came of it. Tempers flared, and Morgan got in his face. We had to pull him off before punches started flying."

"Sounds like no love lost there," my partner murmured.

Jeez, no kidding. Although, after seeing how he acted with Chelsea at our office, it didn't surprise me to hear more about his temper.

Cody agreed. "Pretty much."

"Just one more thing," Caleb said. "Did Morgan have any other activities or hobbies outside of work?"

"Just the usual, the gym, running, beer, good food."

"I guess that does it for now. Thanks for your help. You have given us some great information. If you think of anything else, please reach out to me. Even if it may seem insignificant," Caleb urged.

Cody shook our hands. "Sure man, no problem. If I can help more, don't hesitate to ask. Morgan was like my brother. No one deserves this."

Once he left, Hamilton looked over at me. "What are your thoughts?"

"I think we need to talk to this Theodore Banks. If he and our victim were enemies, he could have a reason to want to cause him harm."

He nodded. "I agree. I will get in contact with him. He could be the break we're looking for."

The next day Caleb set up an interview with Theodore 'Ted' Banks. They agreed to meet at a local pub near the Body by Mimi's corporate office. Paperwork and an appointment at the Wedded Bliss kept me busy all morning, so I just decided to catch up with him there later in the day.

One of the mainstays in Ashford, the Fox and Hound Pub, began as a bar for workers to stop in after a long day at the factories. Over the years it had switched hands, yet always maintained its local working man décor and atmosphere. Now, surrounded by office buildings instead, the bar patrons were more elegant and friendly and less unkempt and rough.

The hostess greeted me when I arrived, and I let her know I was meeting someone. She pointed me towards the booths on the back left side. Caleb noticed me approaching and waved. I slid into the booth next to him, so we both faced the entrance.

He scooted over to make sure I had plenty of room. "Any trouble finding a place to park?"

"Not really." I scanned the room. "I can't remember the last time I was here. Mr. Banks hasn't arrived yet?"

"He texted me about ten minutes before you got here to let me know he was running late."

"Do you think he'll back out?"

Caleb shook his head. "I didn't get that impression."

I set my trusty notepad in front of me and picked up my pen. "While we wait, why don't you go ahead and remind me what we know about him?"

"Ted Banks is friends with Preston Coleman, and he's a co-worker of Morgan's. Specifically, the one who butted heads with our victim."

"We'll need to tread lightly then."

"Correct. Especially since we would prefer he not to run back to his boss and ruin our chances of interviewing him," he pointed out.

We spent another ten minutes going over the notes that Caleb had gathered before our guest arrived.

Theodore Banks was a short, heavy-set man, balding, with a face that resembled a rodent and his eyes were small and dark. He was dressed impeccably in a fine suit, adorned with a gold watch and rings on each hand. Despite his rotund figure, he moved confidently.

"Welcome, I'm Caleb Hamilton. We spoke on the phone. This is my associate, Leah Jordan. Thank you for meeting with us."

He shook our hands. "Not a problem. I apologize for being late."

With a bit of difficulty, I kept a benign expression on my face. The man's warm, sweaty palm grossed me out. He didn't help matters by squeezing my fingers too hard in a predictable attempt at intimidation.

We all sat down and gave him a few minutes to get settled. While our suspect focused his attention on the pretty server who arrived to take our drink order, I discreetly wiped my hand against my slacks. We made small talk about the establishment and its offerings until our order arrived, then the interrogation began.

"Mr. Banks, I understand you are an employee of Coleman Industries. Is that correct?" Caleb asked.

"Yes, nearly twenty-five years now. Please call me Ted," Mr. Banks answered.

"All right. What is your position there?"

"I am a marketing executive for the Body by Mimi brand."

"You worked with Morgan Vanderbilt?"

"Yes, for the past few years," he confirmed.

"How would you describe your relationship?"

"Our relationship? Friendly competitors. We're in the same department, but on different teams. Usually competing against one another," Ted replied.

"Did you two have a relationship outside of the office?"

He took a sip of his drink. "No. Just at work."

"Were there ever any arguments or disagreements between you and Mr. Vanderbilt?" I asked.

Ted shook his head. "Nothing more than the usual. I mean, sometimes my ideas or my team's ideas were better. Sometimes his or his teams were."

"Never anything personal?"

"Exactly. Any minor disagreements at work were trivial and stayed at the office," he explained.

Funny, his answer was different from what Cody told us earlier. Caleb let it go and didn't press further.

"Is there anyone Morgan did have a real problem with or who had an issue with him?"

Ted paused for a moment before he answered. "No one comes to mind. Morgan pretty much stayed to himself. He never hung out with me or my co-workers outside of the office."

Caleb's eyebrows raised. "You didn't find that a little odd?"

The rat man hitched up a shoulder. "Not really. He wasn't the only one. Plus, he was dating the boss's daughter. Maybe he thought it would reflect negatively on him."

"What kind of relationship did you have with Preston Coleman?"

"Good...great I guess you would say. We've been friends for a long time. Even before Mimi's opened and took off."

"Did Mr. Coleman display any special treatment towards any of his employees?" I asked.

Ted shifted in his seat. "If Preston did, he didn't discuss any of that with me. We kept our work relationship professional and our friendship personal. He was a good businessman but shrewd, not the warm and fuzzy type except when it came to his daughter."

I glanced at Caleb and got the nod to keep going. "Speaking of her, let's talk about the night of the rehearsal dinner. Did you speak to Morgan that evening?"

"Yes. We were discussing a project we just finished, and afterward, I went to my table and sat back down with my wife," Ted answered.

"If we talk with her, will she confirm what you've told us?" I asked.

"Of course."

His verbal response stated one thing, but his eyes conveyed something different.

"Sir, is there anything else you remember about Morgan that evening?"

Rat man squinted. "He seemed unlike his usual self."

"Can you elaborate?" Caleb inquired.

"I can't quite pinpoint it, but he appeared upset about something. I thought it was odd, because getting married is a happy occasion, but I brushed it off." He shrugged.

"Did you speak to him anymore that evening?"

Ted shook his head. "No, I didn't."

"Is there anything else you can recall about that night?" Caleb asked.

"Nothing comes to mind. If it does, I will let you know." Morgan's coworker slid out of the booth and stood up.

We exchanged pleasantries and watched as he left.

I turned to look at Caleb. "I think he sounded pretty truthful, don't you?"

My handsome partner took a second before he answered. "He did, but I also feel he may be leaving something out. We should keep him in mind as a person of interest. In the meantime, let's move forward with the other interviews."

CHAPTER ELEVEN

The following morning, Caleb reached out to let me know he set up a meeting with Mrs. Coleman.

"Did you want to come with me?" he asked.

I did, but I hesitated. "It may not be such a good idea with the lawsuit."

He sighed. "True. I forgot about that. Unless you...no, never mind."

"What?" His unfinished sentence piqued my curiosity.

"What if you wear a disguise? A wig, maybe some glasses? From what I've learned about Mrs. Coleman thus far, she's self-absorbed, and I doubt she'd pay very close attention."

He wasn't wrong.

I chuckled. "I think I could scrounge something up. When are we meeting with her?"

"Around three. I can stop by and pick you up on the way," he offered.

What the heck? Why not? "See you then."

After I hung up with Caleb, I went to my bedroom closet and began searching for potential disguises. I had been in such a hurry to relocate when I returned to Ashford, several totes and boxes just got shoved in wherever there was room.

I'd reached the last tub in the stack when I struck gold. My Halloween costume from the previous year lay on top. My old coworkers and I decided to dress up as the cast from Sex in the City. I was Carrie, so the blonde wig would be perfect.

I walked down the hall to my bedroom closet and picked out a very simple pair of black slacks and a navy three-fourth-length sleeve shirt. The bland colors would be ideal since I didn't want to draw attention to myself. I also selected ballet flats to complete the ensemble. The only glasses I had were low-prescription readers, which I never wore. I added them to the outfit.

A couple of hours later, I was dressed and checking the mirror for any last-minute things I needed to fix. My silly appearance made me giggle, but if it fooled Mrs. Coleman, that was all that mattered. I picked up my purse and jacket and waited for Caleb to arrive out front.

When he pulled into the driveway and saw me, his jaw dropped.

I yanked open the passenger door and slid inside.

He busted out laughing. "Jordan? What in the heck?"

I held my hand to my chest, pretending to be offended. "Why, Mr. Hamilton!" I gasped. "How dare you laugh at me. I did the best I could with what I had. The glasses make me look smart, right?"

He grinned. "It's definitely something. What shall I call you?"

Excellent question. "How about Carla?"

"Okay Carla, let's get going."

"Good afternoon. We have an appointment with Mrs. Coleman," Caleb said to the butler, who answered the door.

"Follow me, please. She is expecting you," he stated.

He led us down the long hallway, then turned to his left into what could only be described as the swankiest living room I'd ever seen. A huge silver and crystal chandelier hung in the center of the ceiling and gorgeous leather couches and chairs filled the rest of the space. The walls were a rich creamy tan and several pictures from previous travels adorned them.

"Where should we sit?" I whispered, nudging my partner in the side.

The butler cleared his throat loudly and motioned towards the couch. "Please take a seat. The lady of the house will be with you shortly."

As soon as we sat down, we both took out pens and notebooks, so we'd be prepared when she walked in. The longer we waited, the more nervous I became. My left leg began bouncing slightly. I had met the Colemans before, but between what I had read in the newspapers and how they acted the other night at The Wedded Bliss, they intimidated me. We'd talked to several core people already but weren't any closer to figuring out the identity of the killer than when we started.

Before I knew it, my bouncing grew faster. Caleb reached over and placed his hand on top of my knee. The moment he touched me, it felt like a huge zap of electricity shot through me. I almost yelled out in surprise, but Mrs. Coleman walked in. We both jumped up to greet her.

She floated over to us. "Forgive me for being late, darlings. I had to finish a call with one of the ladies from Junior League. Our next fundraiser is coming up, and I'm the chairperson. Please, have a seat and we'll get started."

She dressed impeccably in a pair of khaki capris, a blue-striped top with a very nautical vibe which worked well with her light complexion and bleach-blonde hair, a white half sweater and tan espadrilles. We both sat down after she did.

An awkward silence filled the room.

Caleb finally broke it. "Mrs. Coleman, thank you for sparing the time out of your busy schedule to talk to us."

"It's an awful thing! My poor Janie is so upset she can't even eat and has no interest in shopping. Such a tragedy. She didn't deserve it," the woman lamented as she reached for a tissue from the side table next to her to dab her eyes and nose.

Um, hello? Morgan didn't either!

Caleb leaned forward. "That is true, which is why we need to find the murderer before he strikes again."

She played the part of the distraught mother to the hilt, and flung her hands in the air, then clasped them against her chest. She paused, and her eyes flew wide. "Wait! Do you think the killer is targeting the rich? Goodness gracious!"

He held out a hand in an attempt to squash her panic. "Now, ma'am, we don't know that. Please calm down. Let's concentrate on what happened to Morgan."

Mrs. Coleman sighed. "I conveyed to her that I didn't approve of that man. No, she wouldn't listen to me, only to her father, of course. He thought he would mentor him, take him under his wing, mold him into a carbon copy of himself. It was just one more thing he could control. If Preston told my daughter the sky was purple, she would trust it. Beautiful she is, but not the brightest, I'm afraid."

"Why do you think Janie and Morgan weren't a good match?" I wondered.

"First of all, a marketing executive? She should marry a CEO like I did. She needs security. Secondly, I simply don't believe he fits in with us. The way he acted sometimes and spoke was not very upper class," she commented.

"How so? Can you explain what you mean, please?" Caleb asked.

"An individual with a good upbringing has a certain air about them, a particular way they carry themselves. I can't describe it more clearly than that. There just is. He was polite enough, but he carried himself like any average person. He wore knockoffs!" She visibly shuddered. "He also purported to have a degree from Yale yet didn't appear to be that knowledgeable. I suggested having him checked out, but my husband wouldn't hear of it."

"Did he know you had objections?" I questioned.

"No. Maybe. I am not aware if he did or not," she answered.

My companion kept going. "At the rehearsal dinner, did you speak to Morgan at all?"

"Briefly, when we first arrived. Then we began greeting guests and talking to some of our friends from the country club."

"How was your soon-to-be son-in-law acting?" I asked.

She shrugged. "Fine, not any different from the usual."

She gave such simple answers to each question. I glanced over at my partner to get a read on what he thought, but it was hard to tell. Though cooperative, Janie's mother appeared rather unconcerned when discussing the actual murder victim.

"Do you remember seeing him at all after the party started before your daughter came to alert you, he was missing?" Caleb inquired.

"We were all busy socializing. I recall he was talking with his groomsmen, then I got pulled into a conversation with the Langfords. Lovely people but

Edwin Langford is a wee bit long-winded if you know what I mean." Mrs. Coleman rolled her eyes.

"Yes, I think we do," I agreed.

My partner tapped his pen thoughtfully on his notebook. "Do you know of anyone who had an issue with Morgan or his relationship besides you?"

She kept fiddling and adjusting the gold bracelets on her left wrist. "Not really. Once Janie rebuffed my attempts to give her advice. I decided if she wanted to make a mistake, then it would be best to let her."

Wow. That was kind of harsh.

I tried a different tactic to see if I could detect anything from her reaction. "Do you believe she would ever harm her fiancé?"

The question appalled her. "Excuse me? Janie? You think she had something to do with this? No! She loved him. I never understood why she did, but she wouldn't hurt anyone."

"Mrs. Coleman, we must be thorough. I know that was a hard question to hear," Caleb explained.

"Why are you asking me such ridiculous things? I thought they had someone in custody?"

He nodded. "They did. However, we have to explore all possibilities."

She lifted her chin, and I could detect the doors of cooperation slamming in our faces. "I believe I've answered your questions. If you'll excuse me, I need to get back to my work. Please, see yourselves out."

After Mrs. Coleman left the room, the butler returned and escorted us out.

"I think you hit a nerve..." I trailed off.

Caleb chuckled. "That's just what we have to do. Shake them up a little."

"She was slightly strange and not the kindest person. I can't believe how much she defended Janie, then turned around and put her down. There was no love lost between her and her future son-in-law," I observed.

"It's bitterness. Not everyone can be so happy-go-lucky. However, I'm not sure I see her risking getting blood on her clothes or exerting herself to murder someone," Caleb mused.

"I don't think that either. She could have hired a person."

"Definitely something to take into consideration."

He checked his watch. "I really need to go back to the office. Do you want to touch base later?"

"Sure. Chelsea and I are going out tonight. We need a girl's night to blow off some steam after such a crappy week."

He chuckled. "You two have fun and stay out of trouble!"

Little did he realize what I had in mind. I felt bad lying, but what he didn't know wouldn't hurt him, right? I did trust Caleb, and we were making progress. but now I was receiving threats. Chelsea had not yet been cleared, and the business was still in danger. I just couldn't wait. We had too much at stake. Interviews were fine, but we needed to act.

"I think we're ready, but let's make sure we have everything first. Flashlights?" I asked.

She raised two black Maglites. "Check."

"Gloves?"

"Check."

"Ski masks?"

Chelsea held one in each hand and waved them in confirmation. "Check."

"Cheez-Its?"

"Check... wait, what did you say?"

"Cheez-Its. We have to keep up our energy, duh!" I frowned and glared at her in mock irritation.

She laughed and shook her head. "Leah, you are such a goofball."

"Bite me," I responded with a giggle.

"So, what is the plan?" Chelsea asked.

"Morgan was living in those new condominiums on the other side of town. They have a private back entrance. We'll wait 'til midnight and take your car since it's dark blue, park a couple blocks away and head to his place."

"I think you've watched too many true crime shows, Leah. What if we get caught? I could have my bail revoked. You could be arrested, too."

"What if we don't? My business—our business is on the line and so is our reputation. If we can't prove who the real killer is, everyone will remember the Wedded Bliss as nothing more than a crime scene. Who in their right mind would want to get married at one of those?"

"I understand what you're saying, but I thought that's why Caleb was working with you so he could handle this kind of stuff?" she asked.

"Pfft. No. Now someone is threatening me. I'm not letting it go. Are you with me or against me?" I replied.

My friend grew quiet and paused a moment before she answered. "With you," she agreed reluctantly. "If we do get caught, I won't hold back from uttering the 'I told you so's'."

"Deal. Let's finish getting ready."

An hour later, we were finally in her car. I rode shotgun so I could navigate. The tension in the air was palpable. I might have talked big earlier, but deep down I was very nervous.

We entered the condominiums and cut the headlights. Studying the map, we decided to park on Peachtree Street. It was close, but not too close. Our victim lived two streets over on Passion Fruit Lane. She parked the car along the curb away from any streetlamps. Shouldering our backpacks, we headed off.

As we approached Cherry Street behind Morgan's condo, we both breathed huge sighs of relief. So far, so good. Once we reached the rear of the condo unit which backed up to his, we crouched down and scampered along the wall to avoid being seen. The two of us kept creeping until my friend's muffled scream froze me in my tracks.

"What? What?" I whispered loudly. "Are you okay?"

"No! I just face-planted into a spider web," Chelsea replied.

"Eww. We're almost there. It's too late to turn back now," I reminded her.

Chelsea brushed her face off, and we kept going. "Spiders are one thing, but if we come across anything else creepy crawly, I may have to re-think this friendship."

We were only two houses down from Morgans when a little dog started barking at us. Crap! I knelt beside the fence and stuck a couple of fingers through the slats. Maybe if it smelled me and saw that I was friendly, it would calm down. I felt the cold nose run across them. Oh, thank God.

"Nice puppy, sweet puppy," I cooed. I began to withdraw my hand when the little snot bit down on my index finger! "Sonofa--!"

It started barking again. If the little monster refused to quiet down, it would wake up the whole neighborhood, and we would surely be caught.

"Are you all right? Leah, what should we do?"

"I'll be fine. He avoided breaking the skin. Hand me the Cheez-Its stat!" I ordered.

She grabbed the crackers from her backpack and tossed them to me. I ripped open the box and began pouring some over the fence. Hoping that would be enough, Chelsea and I slowly crept away. We reached Morgan's back patio without any further issues and surveyed the area to make sure the coast was clear.

We found ourselves on a cement slab populated with a small table and umbrella, two metal chairs and a covered grill. Several potted plants lined either side of the steps. Very simple. I reached to check the door handle. It refused to move. Darn.

"Well?" she asked from behind me.

"It's locked. Help me look for a key." Most people in Cherry Hollow still didn't lock their doors, and if they did, there was always a spare around. She began searching the table and chairs while I headed to the grill. I ran my fingers over the metal frame, the hood and the underside, to no avail.

"Nada. You have any luck, Leah?" Chelsea asked.

"I'll inspect the plants if you examine the patio perimeter. Maybe one of the rocks is a fake." Bending down, I picked up the smallest pot first. I tried to cover every inch and even dug down into the dirt. Nothing. I used the same technique on the next two pots but got the same result.

The last, and the largest. was filled with red geraniums and a small frog sculpture. I felt around the bottom and sides and came up empty. I lifted the amphibian out and turned to set it on the step. Clink. Clink. I paused, afraid it had broken. Noticing no visible cracks or breaks, I picked it up again and shook it. Clink, clink, clink. I ran my hands over it and located a little button. Once I pressed it, a door popped open, and inside was a key. Bingo! I took the key out and replaced the figurine in the pot.

"Found it! Come on," I whispered loudly to Chelsea.

We headed to the door, where I inserted it into the lock and turned. Success! I cracked it, waiting to see if an alarm would sound. Silence. I slid it open the rest of the way, and we hurried inside.

We entered the minimalist eat-in kitchen. The dining area was set up as if anticipating guests. We continued into the living room. A brown faux leather couch sat against the wall to the left with a matching recliner beside it on the right. A huge flat-screen television was mounted above the impressive marble fireplace.

It looked like one of those models for a housing development, not an actual home. It felt very impersonal. Either Morgan was an expert house-keeper, or he didn't want people to become familiar with him. He could spend all his time with Janie and was never home, but my senses told me something was off. I made a mental note for later.

Chelsea followed me through the living room and around the bend to the stairwell. I glanced at her and pointed up. We crept upstairs and stopped. The closest two doors stood open. We saw a bedroom to the right, a bathroom catty-corner from us and a couple more rooms further down the hall on the left side.

We checked the sleeping quarters and found it was simply that, Morgan's room. Moving on, we passed the lavatory and headed for the second bedroom. I shone my flashlight inside and realized it was a home office. A massive desk sat centered in the rear, flanked by two large file cabinets and wood bookshelves on the right wall.

"Let's start here," I whispered. "You can have the shelves and cabinets." I went toward the elegant dark cherry desk.

"Sounds good," Chelsea replied, approaching the shelves first.

No knickknacks, pictures of family or friends - let alone one of Janie - resided upon its surface. Only a calendar, a couple of pens and a yellow legal pad could be seen. I took a seat in the high-backed leather chair and opened the left drawer.

Envelopes, stamps, rubber bands, and paper clips. I removed all the items just to make sure there wasn't anything else. It was empty. Carefully placing everything back in and closing it, I moved on to the next one. Legal pads, pencils, and more pens. Man, I was striking out.

I returned all the contents and closed it, but it became stuck. Reaching my hand in, my fingers met with the corner of an envelope. I got a better grasp on it and yanked it out. Straightening it, I noticed the return address was Cherry Hollow Savings and Loan. It appeared to be a bank statement.

Even though it was against the law to read someone else's mail, it was already opened, so it didn't count, right?

I pulled the document out, unfolded it, and skimmed over it. Most of what I saw were your typical charges, gas, groceries, etc. However, several large deposits to his account caught my eye Five thousand dollars, ten thousand and the last one a couple of weeks ago for twenty grand!

Each deposit was made in cash. Marketing was a good career, but even I knew they didn't make that much in a month. I reached into my book bag, pulled out my cell phone and took a picture of the dates and amounts of the transactions. My best friend had grown quiet.

I turned around. "Find anything?"

"Not really. Most of the files in this file cabinet are for bills, utilities, cell phones et cetera. I still have one more to go. What about you?" Chelsea asked.

"Something is definitely going on, just not sure what it is yet," I replied.

I returned to searching. The deep bottom drawer on the left yielded only a tan metal lockbox. I lifted it up and placed it in front of me. Its light weight made me wonder if it contained anything at all. It boasted a single lock, which I studied after I tried to open it without success.

I plucked a paper clip from the desk, unbent it, and attempted to unlock it. After placing it in further, I moved it around. It wouldn't budge. They sure made it look much easier on television. Maybe I need an additional one. I grabbed a second, straightened it out, and stuck them both in the lock. After a few minutes of poking and prodding, it still didn't unlock. I snatched up the letter opener and shoved it between the top and bottom lids. I twisted and wrenched it until it popped.

Inside the lockbox, I found a passport, driver's license, and credit cards. The pictures on the documents looked just like our victim, but the name on them read 'Jason Eakins' from Cincinnati, Ohio. If he wasn't Morgan Vanderbilt, then who was he really? This Jason person?

"Chels, I think you should look at this."

She turned around and leaned over my left shoulder.

"Wait, that is him! Why does it say his first name is Jason?" she asked.

"That's what I'm wondering. I just need to finish writing all this down." I wrote the last digit down from the license when a loud disturbance came from downstairs.

"Leah! What was that?"

"I don't know. Hurry up and let's put everything back where we found it."

She tidied up the bookshelves while I returned all the belongings to the lockbox and placed it in the drawer, trying not to make any noise.

Motioning to Chelsea, we both cut off our flashlights, threw our backpacks on and crept towards the door. I moved forward, listening to see if I picked up on anything. Not a peep. I pointed to the stairs and let her walk ahead. I followed. Halfway down the staircase, we heard a thump. I shoved her down the rest of the steps.

"Go! I'll catch up," I hissed.

Chelsea looked back at me, unsure whether to leave me. I motioned for her to keep going. She yanked open the front door and ran. My heart raced, and I tightened my grip on my book bag, ready to use it as a weapon. So, it wasn't much of a threat, but I had to work with what I had.

I heard a tiny sound behind me and whipped my head around. Peering up the steps, I saw a masked figure in all black standing at the top. The only things visible were the eyes. Our gazes locked, and before I could scream, the person rushed down the stairs toward me. They shoved past me, causing me to fall back and hit my head on the banister.

Everything went black.

chapter twelve

What felt like only a few minutes later, I opened my eyes. Ugh, my skull throbbed something fierce. Removing my gloves, I reached my left hand up to cradle my head when my fingers made contact with a sticky substance. I brought them to my nose and inhaled. The metallic odor of blood filled my nostrils. Great, just great. Wobbly and woozy, with my brain pounding, I managed to stand up and staggered to the front door.

As I reached out to grab the handle, light streaming in from the window reflected on my watch. I pushed the little button on the right side to make the face light up. The display read 1 a.m. Chelsea must have been freaking out. Half stumbling, half limping, I left the condo, closing the door behind me, making sure to wipe off any prints.

I reached the sidewalk and surveyed my surroundings. The night remained dark and quiet. My body made me aware of numerous bone-bruising aches as I tottered across the street to the car. Chelsea jumped out and ran over to me.

"Oh, my god! Where have you been? Don't you know you scared the living crap out of me? Never do that again!" She pulled me into a tight hug, and I groaned.

"Looser, looser please," I managed to squeak out.

She released me. "I'm sorry, but I thought you were dead. Are you okay?"

"No. Whoever was in that house was not happy we were there. He knocked me down and ran out past me. I ended up passing out, my ribs might be broken, and I may have a concussion. Plus, I might need stitches."

"Oh, Leah. Did you get a look at your attacker?"

"No. It was too dark. All I could tell is that they were dressed in all dark-colored clothing," I answered.

"What should we do? Take you to the ER?" she asked.

"I think that's a great idea," I responded as she assisted me into the passenger seat and made sure I buckled up.

Chelsea climbed in behind the wheel.

"We can't tell anyone about this, especially not Caleb," I mumbled, clutching my aching head as she drove.

"Why not?"

"Because we were breaking the law. I don't think either of us would look good in orange, do you?"

She winced. "Hmm, valid point. Which hospital?"

"Go to St. Anthony's."

"What are you going to tell them when we arrive?" she asked.

"I'll simply say I'm a clumsy fool and fell down some stairs." My bruises screamed at me when she hit a pothole. "Ow! Please, hurry."

The pounding in my head killed me, and my left side felt so tender, I kept having to adjust the seat belt. By the time we reached the emergency entrance, I swore everything was spinning. Luckily, she managed to get me from the car to the registration desk.

Unlike hospitals in most other towns, St. Anthony's was pretty fast. They got me back to triage and in an exam room right away. X-rays, five stitches, wrapped ribs, really good pain meds, aftercare instructions and two hours later, we were ready to go. I signed my release papers and Chelsea wheeled me through the hall to the lobby. The medication took effect, and I started to zone out.

Suddenly, I felt the chair speed up, and we went flying around the next corner. My eyes popped open as my hands clenched the armrests in a death grip.

"Girl, slow down!" I exclaimed.

"Just go with it..." she muttered through gritted teeth, the rest of it unintelligible. "It's him, it's him!" She tossed her head back over her shoulder.

"Him? Caleb? Oh crap!" What was he doing here? My best friend continued shoving me along like we were in a race, almost dumping me from the wheelchair when she did a wheelie. My stomach grew queasy.

"Leah? Hey, hold on!" he called from behind us.

"Stop!" I exclaimed.

She brought us to a screeching halt.

The floor below me looked a lot closer than it had before. I closed my eyes, covered my face, and waited for the inevitable thud. It never came. Wait a minute, I hit something. Solid, but also warm and smelled faintly like men's cologne. I opened them and glanced up. Caleb helped me back into the wheelchair.

"Oh, hi." Jeez, I sounded ridiculous.

"What happened?" he asked.

"Not much, just a couple of minor injuries. Nothing that a little rest and medication won't help."

"A couple? You look like you've been in a bar fight," he commented.

Gee, thanks a lot. As if I didn't already feel awful. I grew very self-conscious and reached up nervously, tucking my hair behind my left ear.

"Like she said, just some minor injuries," my best friend piped up.

"Nice to see you, too," I replied, attempting to give him a half smile.

He glanced at Chelsea, then back at me. "Okay, you two, cut the crap. What actually happened?"

"Why should I tell you?" I grumbled.

"I'm asking, and I'm concerned," Caleb said.

"Concerned? I am a grown woman. I. Can. Take. Care. Of. Myself." I started to get annoyed. My head felt fuzzy, my stomach did flip-flops, and I really wanted to be curled up in my own bed.

"I know that. Earlier when we spoke, you mentioned you were staying in. Obviously, that's a lie. You weren't snooping, were you?" He looked me right in the eye.

"No. I told you I would stop. Honestly, I just took a bad fall, Leah the klutz, that's me. Tell him, Chels," I pleaded.

"It's true. We were having a girl's night in, dancing and being goofy, and she tripped over one of the cats."

Yeah, that seemed plausible. Did I look like a dancer? If looks could kill, she would have been kaput!

"Please, just get the car, and I'll finish talking to him," I urged my best friend.

"Right, sure. Be back shortly." As Chelsea passed me, she mouthed the words 'I'm sorry'.

"So, tell me what really happened?" Caleb faced me with his arms crossed.

Even frustrated, he looked sexy. This wasn't the moment to press his buttons further.

"We were taking a walk, and we may have ended up in Morgan's neighborhood," I replied, trying to avoid looking him in the eye.

His eyebrows raised. "You two just happened to 'walk' all the way across town for an evening stroll? I wasn't aware you were so committed to your health."

I shrugged my shoulders. "I'm complex. What can I say?"

His voice lowered. "I know you didn't inflict the injuries yourself. Who did?"

"I don't know. That's the truth. We were upstairs in Morgan's office and heard noises. Once they stopped, Chelsea and I decided to take our leave. She made it out, but when I turned around, the intruder shoved past me, which caused me to tumble down the stairs."

"What were you two thinking? It could have ended much, much worse. Not to mention the rules both of you violated. What if you had gotten arrested?" Another expression of worry washed over Caleb's face.

"Really, we're both fine." I hoped to alleviate some of his concerns.

My friend pulled up in front of the doors and cut short our conversation.

He sighed and gave my shoulder a gentle pat. "Go home, get some rest. We'll talk in the morning. No more snooping!"

Chelsea hopped out of the car and opened the passenger door while Caleb wheeled me out.

Once we got to my house, she helped me inside and got me settled on the couch. She placed bottled water, my pain medicine and my cell phone within reach on the coffee table. Then it was lights out.

The next morning, I woke up to the sounds of pots and pans clanging around in my kitchen. Aww, she was the best. How sweet of her to make me breakfast! I threw my blankets off and tried sitting up. My head got woozy, so I laid back down. I made another much slower but successful attempt and padded off towards the kitchen.

"Chelsea, you are a gem! You really didn't have to do this," I said, taking a seat at the table.

The open fridge door hid her. My stomach grumbled. The wonderful aroma of eggs and bacon filled my nostrils. Luckily, there was already a plate of fresh blueberry muffins sitting out. I pilfered one, pulled it apart, and started nibbling.

"Hey, you're awake!"

The deep voice surprised me. I choked on my bite and dropped the remainder of my muffin. My head snapped up, and there stood Caleb.

I coughed and sputtered, "You're certainly not Chelsea! What are you doing here?"

"Good morning to you, too. I sent her home to get some rest. She was exhausted from staying up all night watching over you. So, I offered to take over," he smiled, leaning against my counter holding a half gallon of orange juice.

He appeared incredibly attractive in a pair of tight rugged blue jeans and a close-fitting gray T-shirt. Here I was with my hair sticking up all over the place, feeling bloated and looking like crap.

I cocked my head as I gazed at him. "You cook?"

Caleb brought over a plate filled with crispy bacon, scrambled eggs and pancakes and placed it in front of me. It smelled divine. He took a seat across from me at the table.

"My mom was all about gender equality. Just because I am a male, didn't mean I couldn't learn to prepare meals and clean. She always wanted me and my siblings to be independent and self-sufficient. "I'm no Emeril Lagasse, but no one usually complains when I whip up something in the kitchen," he responded with a smile.

"Smart, good looking, and you can cook. Who would've thunk it?" I declared, stabbing into the pile of pancakes.

"Haha. Enough about me. Let's talk about you and what happened last night." Before he could finish his next thought, I shoved a huge bite into my mouth.

"Mmm...mmm," I mumbled, shaking my head.

Caleb smirked. "I'll wait."

I hurried up and swallowed. "Fine. I wanted to learn some more about Morgan, so I went snooping."

"Why didn't you call me? I would have gone with you."

"No, you would have tried to talk me out of it. This is my life, my business in jeopardy. You'll finish the investigation and go on. The Wedded Bliss could be ruined. I just can't let everything my mom and my Aunt Sissy worked so hard for to be taken away."

"Leah, if you're killed, too, it won't make a difference. Don't you get that? Whomever we are searching for is not pleased we're investigating this."

"I know." Now I was getting frustrated.

"I know you know, but you need to let me handle this from here on out. It's too dangerous," Caleb urged.

"I'm not making any promises," I replied as I scooped up a forkful of eggs.

"You're not intending to listen to me, are you?"

"We'll see," I responded by shoving more into my mouth.

"Are you at least planning to share what you found out last night?" he asked, staring at me.

"What I can tell you thus far is that I don't believe Morgan is the handsome, well-off, cookie cutter businessman individuals thought he was."

"Who really is who we think they are these days?"

"I stumbled upon some identification cards with a different name, and I wrote it down. Could you run it for me?" I reached for my book bag sitting in the chair to my right and pulled out one of the pages from last night's notebook. I handed it to him.

He studied it and raised an eyebrow. "Interesting. That would explain why Morgan Vanderbilt didn't really exist up until a few years ago. What else you got?"

"He wasn't much of a pack rat or very sentimental. Morgan's condominium was sparsely decorated. It reminded me of the model homes you see at housing developments."

"Are you going to manage if I go in a bit? I should follow up on a few things."

"Fine with me. Did Chelsea mention if she planned to come back?"

"I believe she said she would call you later."

A wave of wooziness hit me yet again. "Okay great. I think I'll rest for a bit."

Caleb nodded. "Good idea. I'll clean up."

I gave him a grateful smile. "Thank you for the meal and looking after me. You really didn't need to."

"I wanted to. Plus, next time you can take care of me," he said with a wink.

I finished the rest of my breakfast and carried the dishes over to the sink. Heading into the living room, I noticed the cats were still stretched out on the couch, soaking up sunbeams. I curled up on the opposite end and tossed a blanket over myself.

I woke up a little while later, dazed and confused. When I sat up and felt a stabbing pain shoot through my side, it all came back to me. I looked around but didn't see Caleb. I called out his name and was met with silence. As I reached for my glass of water, I found a note:

Jordan-
Had to head out. Call you later. Stay out of trouble!
-C

I placed my drink on the table. The next thing I knew, I heard someone beating on my front door.

"Hang on! I'm coming!" I exclaimed as I heaved my aching body off the sofa.

I unlocked the deadbolt and cracked the door just wide enough to peer out with one eye. Two men dressed in very nice dress suits and ties stood on the other side. Did the cops find out about last night? Crap! Play it cool, Leah, play it cool.

"Good morning, ma'am! How are you doing today?" the taller one said first with the second guy chiming in.

I didn't know which was worse, opening the door to begin with, or the headache their cheery voices gave me.

"Fine," I responded, deciding to keep my answers short and sweet.

"Wonderful! We're with the Church of Anointed Saints and are out spreading the gospel and inviting people to visit our church," the tall man explained.

"Do you currently attend services?" the shorter one asked.

"You know what? I'm not really feeling well this morning. Why don't you just leave your information, and I can contact you later."

I grabbed the pamphlet out of the smaller guy's hand and shut the door. Tossing it down on the hallway table, I stumbled back to the couch.

A couple of hours passed, and sitting around wasn't accomplishing anything. There was stuff I needed to get done at The Wedded Bliss. A few stitches and sore ribs weren't going to keep me down. I found my cell phone and dialed Chelsea's number.

"Hey, it's me. Are you able to come pick me up?" I asked when she answered.

"Leah, I thought the doctor told you to relax. We can cover things so you can rest."

"I can't sit around anymore. Let me get dressed, do something with my hair and take my meds. I'll wait for you out front."

We hung up and I made my way down the hall to my room. I chose a pair of black yoga pants and a loose-fitting, blue, short-sleeved button-up top. It took me longer than usual, but my ribs were so tender, it made lifting my arms difficult.

Chelsea arrived and got me to the office. Once she had me settled and brought me everything I needed, she left to head to hers. I picked up my phone messages and began flipping through them. Sales call, sales call, Cherry Hollow Gazette, and a follow-up call from Eva over at Buds and Bouquets. I pulled my notebook out and plucked out the page I took from Morgan's legal pad.

I twisted the knob on my small desk lamp and held the paper up to the light. Sure enough, a faint impression of a few characters and what looked like some numbers were visible.

I plucked a pencil out of my middle drawer and rubbed it gently over the page. Slowly the letters formed. 'Mtg at 3456 Potter Avenue. Back lot. CA'. It was a reminder of some kind.

I turned to my computer and opened the browser window and typed in 'CA'. Of course, a gazillion results popped up. Shoot. How would I narrow this down? Setting the paper aside, I flipped through my notebook, to a fresh page, and wrote down everything we learned last night. Morgan's other name, the identification cards I found, and the meeting memo.

Hmm, let's try something else. I cleared the search bar and typed in the alias plus the initials, 'CA'. The first result of relevance displayed an article about Justin Hanover from San Diego, CA. The picture that accompanied it showed an older man, not Morgan. I kept scrolling through the results but got nowhere and decided I needed a break.

CHAPTER THIRTEEN

The bridesmaids were the hardest witnesses to nail down for interviews. We spoke with Addie and Maddie Tennant first. Childhood friends of Janie's, the sisters were like peas in a pod, and insisted we meet with them together.

Killing two birds with one stone, I asked them to come pick up some of the miscellaneous items that belonged to Janie. With all the chaos on the night of the rehearsal, everyone exited in a hurry, and they were left behind. I arranged for Caleb to meet me at The Wedded Bliss that afternoon. He arrived in time to help me get ready for the questioning.

In the Cupid Room, I made sure to have iced tea, water, and cookies on the table while he brought over four chairs from the stacks along the end wall.

We took seats, and I set out my trusty notepad and pen. I wondered if we'd have to wait long, but they arrived on time.

Sally escorted the women in right at two o'clock. We exchanged pleasantries, and they sat down across from us.

My partner started. "First off, I want to thank you ladies for coming in. I know these past few days have been hard. We really hope that you are able to assist with any information you have."

"Janie is our BFF. We'll do anything to help," they both chimed in.

"Great. Why don't you start by telling me about what happened after the rehearsal lunch on Friday? Addie, you can go first." he prompted.

"It was awesome. We headed to the spa and were pampered from head to toe. They have the best hot stone massages, and the mud mask facials are divine. We even had champagne with strawberries. Some of us may have had a little too much of the bubbly," she giggled.

"How was the bride? Was she enjoying herself?"

"She was having a great time. She has been waiting for the day forever," the bridesmaid emphasized each syllable of the last word.

"Were there any issues between her and her fiancé leading up to the wedding rehearsal?" Caleb asked.

"No. Just typical relationship stuff," Addie answered.

I glanced up from my notepad. "What do you mean by typical?"

"You know, if she went shopping too much, Morgan would complain, and if he worked a lot of overtime, she would get annoyed."

"Did their arguments ever turn violent?" I asked.

She shook her head. "Oh no, nothing like that. He was all talk and no action. Within hours she was back on his good side, and they were making up."

"Did you see the groom on Friday?" I questioned.

"Yes. We were all dancing and drinking," she responded.

Caleb turned to her twin. "What about you Maddie? Anything to add?"

Addie's sister shrugged her shoulders. "Not really. We only knew him through Janie. If she was happy, we were, too. He treated her well, took care of her and that's all you truly wish for your dear friend. Anytime we were around him was pleasant."

"Is there anyone you can think of that would want bad things to happen to him?" I asked.

She fiddled with the ring on her finger. "No, no one."

My partner cleared his throat. "Would his fiancée have a motive to injure him?"

Maddie's jaw dropped. "How could you even ask that?"

"I know it's hard to hear, but often in a murder, the killer is usually an individual close to the victim," Caleb explained.

"She doesn't have a murderous bone in her body. She may be a little snobby and spoiled, but she would never hurt someone else," Addie interjected.

"Noted. Maddie is there anything further you can think of that I need to know?" he asked.

"Well, there is one thing, but not sure if it's a big deal…" her voice trailed off.

"Go on," Caleb urged.

"A few weeks after their engagement announcement was published in the newspapers, Janie's ex-fiancé showed up," the bridesmaid replied.

"Oh really?" My partner raised an eyebrow.

Addie reached over to smack her sister's arm and hissed. "Hush! Janie swore us to secrecy." She glanced over at my partner and me. "It's not significant."

Maddie rolled her eyes at her sister.

"Please, don't hold back. What's his name?" Caleb urged.

"Dalton McVay. The two of them dated forever. They met at Milton Academy, were high school sweethearts and he graduated at the top of his class. He also came from a wealthy family, and they belonged to the same country club as her parents. Everyone was sure they would be married and have kids by now."

Wow. Sounds like the kind of guy Mrs. Coleman would have been proud to call her son-in-law.

"What caused them to split up?" I questioned.

"He went away to Lambert University, and let's just say, he had way too much fun. Janie remained local at Otterbein University. She wouldn't put up with his partying ways, and she dumped him before their senior year," Maddie explained.

The rich daddy's girl attended college. I was shocked. "How did he take the break-up?"

"Not so well. He was very bitter and begged her to come back. She stood her ground though."

He sounded pretty messed up over the split. "Do you think he would ever want to harm her or her fiancé?"

"Hmm. To be honest, I'm not sure. She casually mentioned he was in town. She did say he was trying to talk her out of going through with the wedding," Maddie replied.

"Was Morgan aware of that?" Caleb asked.

Addie leaned forward. "I don't know. Janie failed to bring it up. Mr. Coleman loved him. Dalton's parents and the Coleman's were friends who went way back. I guess her fiancé could have found out."

"Ladies, I want to thank you for your time. I think that's enough for today. If there is anything else, you might have seen, heard, or witnessed in the last few days up until now that seemed off, or you may have forgotten to mention, please contact me," Caleb said.

"If you girls pull your car around back, we have the items that were left here ready to be loaded. I'll have Steven haul the cart to the rear door, and he'll be happy to help you load it," I instructed.

"Thank you. I'm sure Janie will appreciate it," Addie answered.

"No problem at all. Please let us know if there is anything else you need," I responded.

The two left the room while Caleb and I stayed back to decompress.

"Now, that was much better than I could have imagined," I murmured.

"I agree," he replied as he flipped through the notes. "Not only did we learn of another potential suspect, but he seems to have one hell of a motive to want Morgan out of the way."

I nodded. "Love does tend to make you do crazy things."

"Indeed. I can return to my hotel room and run a quick background on Mr. McVay and see if anything pops."

"Sounds great. I should get caught up on some paperwork before home. We'll catch up tomorrow?" I asked.

"Yep. I'll buzz you then," Caleb replied as he headed out.

My alarm sounded the next morning, and I stretched my arm out to turn it off. I rolled back over, and my cell phone began to ring. Whining, I leaned over and plucked it from my nightstand.

"Hello?" I answered, my voice husky.

"Leah, sorry, did I wake you?" our secretary's tone came over the line.

"Is everything okay?" I asked.

"No. You need to come to the office now!"

I glanced over at the clock. It was only eight A.M.

"I'm sure whatever it is can wait another hour until I get in," I hedged.

"It can't. The Wedded Bliss has been defaced. It's terrible!" Sally exclaimed, her voice growing frantic.

"Vandalized?" I shot straight up in bed. "How bad is it? Oh my God! Do Chelsea and Meg know?"

"I haven't told them yet. You're the first one I called. Can you come? I'm going to call the police."

"I'll be right there." I hung up the phone, threw on some clothes, tossed food in the girls' bowls, and ran out of the house.

As I pulled into the parking area, my jaw hit the floor. The sign on the building was fractured and cracked. Some awful person had broken several windows and sprayed graffiti all over the walls and doors.

My poor, distraught secretary paced around outside.

She waved her arm toward the front of the building. "Horrible, isn't it? Who would do such a thing?"

I wanted to cry. It looked awful. "Yes, yes, it is. I have no idea. Are the cops coming? Have you been inside yet?"

"Yes, they said they would send someone over. No, I decided to wait for you. I didn't want to go in alone," Sally answered, rubbing her arms as she tried to comfort herself.

"Good. Let's check it out together and see if anything else is damaged. I could really do with a cup of coffee, and I'm sure you could, too. It'll help calm you," I suggested.

"I could use some. My nerves are a little frazzled right now," Sally agreed.

I wrapped my arm around her, and we walked in the front door. We filled our mugs and went to the conference room as we waited for the cops to arrive.

A couple of cups of coffee later, we heard a buzz at the main door. She and I rushed to answer it. I opened it and came face to face with Luke Strickland. His handsome face showed great concern as his gorgeous blue eyes met mine. My heart fluttered. For the briefest moment, I forgot about the dreadful event at hand.

Sally poked my elbow. I blinked and coughed while my face grew annoyingly warm.

"Morning, please come in," I said, stepping back to let him enter.

He nodded and plucked a small notepad from his light gray jacket pocket. "Ladies. I'm here to take a report on the vandalism."

"Slow day in the office? Don't they usually just send a patrol officer for this kind of stuff?" I quipped.

Sally nudged me hard in the side.

"I was already over this way, but I can go if you want me to," Luke responded. "With everything that has happened recently, we're pretty busy, and a lot of the guys are pulling double duty."

I felt like a jerk. I hadn't meant to be a smart ass, but emotions were sky-high lately.

"Sorry, it's early, and it's been a lousy day so far," I said, hoping my apology would suffice.

My secretary gave me a look, then turned towards Luke and smiled. "We're glad you're here."

The detective laced his thumbs through his belt loops. "I already have one of our officers taking photographs of the exterior, while I gather some information from you. Have you noticed any interior damage?"

"We haven't seen anything so far," Sally responded.

"We do need to inspect the building. When we came in, we headed straight to the breakroom and then the conference room. We didn't want to disturb any possible evidence," I explained.

"I appreciate it. I'll conduct a brief survey of the building, while you two examine the offices. Let me know if anything is missing or seems out of place. We need to use a hands-off approach. If you see something, yell, and I will come examine it," Luke instructed.

We nodded our acknowledgment. I examined mine and Chelsea's while Sally inspected Meg's and Chef Stefan's. Everything appeared undisturbed in the two I checked. I waited in the hall until she finished.

"Notice anything out of place?" I asked her when she returned to the hallway.

"No, thankfully. It seems all things here were good," she replied.

"Great. Let's go find Luke and let him know," I said.

We returned to the front of the building. Once we stepped outside, we saw him talking to another officer.

"All done?" he asked as we approached.

"Yep. Everything appears to be fine inside," I answered.

"That's good. I just want to ask you ladies some questions. Do you have any idea who might have wanted to do this?"

"Not at all. We've been here for over twenty years and never experienced something like this before," Sally said.

"Leah?" Luke turned his gaze towards me.

"I cannot think of anyone specifically, but do you think it could be related to Morgan's murder?" I wondered.

"It could. You never know. We'll have to examine all the evidence before we have more information. My guys just need to finish a few more photographs and gather the rest of the data. Hopefully, they have located some fingerprints and be able to connect this to a suspect."

"What happens now?" I asked.

"Once we're finished, you can start cleaning up. I would also advise you to reach out to your insurance company and see if it's possible to file a claim for any of the damage. Let me give you, my card. The report should be filed either later today or tomorrow. You follow up with the department and should be able to request a copy within the next forty-eight hours."

"That's good to know, thank you." I took it and placed it in my pocket as Luke headed back outside.

He squeezed my elbow. "Be careful, okay? I don't like worrying about you."

Butterflies fluttered around in my chest. "I will," I promised.

I turned to my secretary after watching him walk away to speak to one of the evidence techs.

"Why don't I call Chelsea and Meg, fill them in on what happened, reach out to the insurance agent and set up a glass repair company to come out? In the meantime, will you please gather up some trash bags, brooms and dustpans, so that when we get an all-clear, we can start cleaning up?" I asked.

"Sure. I'll grab whatever I find," Sally replied.

I went to my office and called the two girls. They were both already on their way. My second call to our insurance was tedious but necessary to get the ball rolling. I lucked out and found a glass repair company in Aunt Sissy's old Rolodex. Murray's Windows and Glass would send over a technician to take information and photos so they could draw up an estimate. As I finished up, Meg stuck her head into my office door.

"Hey, Leah, we're here."

"Great. I was finishing up some calls. Let's go meet up with the other ladies."

We walked up to reception.

Sally saw us as we approached the front desk. "Perfect timing. The officers just left. Where should we begin?"

"Meg and I can begin by cleaning up the larger glass fragments," Chelsea offered.

"I'll start sweeping," Sally said, grabbing one of the brooms and a dustpan.

"That works. I'm going to see if I can scrub off the spray paint," I replied. "Let's get to work."

It took a few hours and a lot of sweat, but The Wedded Bliss was looking so much better. The glass company had come and gone and would email their estimate when it was ready. John, our maintenance guy, was already working on changing the locks simply as a precaution.

I asked the other ladies to meet me in the conference room when we were finished. "I want to begin by thanking all of you for jumping in and helping clean up the aftermath. Not exactly how we planned to start the day, but I am so glad you guys are here."

"Of course, dear. Family helps one another," Sally said.

"I know, but I can't help feeling like this is all my fault," I replied, anxiously twisting my fingers.

"Why would you say that?" Chelsea questioned.

"Yeah, people are dumb," Meg scoffed. "How can you be responsible?"

I placed both of my hands on either side of my face and shook my head. "There is obviously someone who is not thrilled I am looking into Morgan's murder."

"Now, now, don't blame yourself. No one got hurt. Whoever did this is just scared and acting out to draw attention elsewhere," our secretary advised.

"I know, you're probably right. It's not going to deter me, though," I replied.

"Good. I hope not. But you need to be extra careful," she cautioned.

"Why don't we all get some lunch, revitalize, and try to return to normal?" I suggested as everyone began to disperse.

"Nothing has been ordinary lately. I'm not sure if I know of what you speak?" Chelsea smirked.

After eating and returning calls that were overdue for follow-up after the morning's incident, I decided to try my hand at painting over the graffiti. No matter how hard I scrubbed earlier, the glaring obscenities didn't budge and stuck out like a sore thumb on the building. Last year, Aunt Sissy had

The Wedded Bliss exterior re-painted and as luck would have it, she made sure they left extra cans. I headed to the basement and found a couple of paintbrushes, a roller, a tray and a ladder.

It required a few trips, but I finally got everything gathered. Once outside, I plugged my earbuds into my cell phone, and started listening to my Top 40s station. Nothing like a little music to kick things off. I poured some paint, took one of the rollers and loaded it up.

An upbeat song by Pink came on, and I was in my groove. I carried the tray up the ladder and set it on the shelf. I rolled over a section and watched the letters slowly disappear with each swipe across, boogieing as I went. I'd almost finished, but a small portion about "6 x 6" remained on the top left.

As I reached forward, my shirt snagged on the right upper corner of the ladder. I kept on struggling and pulling, making one last firm attempt to get loose. My body jerked backward, and my hands slipped off the ladder. The combination of movements put me off balance.

"Oh no, Leah!" the voice called as I fell. Luke dashed across the short distance to reach me and caught me just before I hit the concrete. "Are you all right?" he asked.

The real concern in his eyes made me all mushy inside. I quickly glanced away. My cheeks grew warm with embarrassment.

"Uh yeah, I think so. More shaken up than anything else," I said, grasping his arm to steady myself as he set me on my feet. "Good thing you were here. I thought you'd left by now." I never realized how strong and muscular he'd grown. Growing up as kids, we always knew him as just Meg's annoying, bossy, older brother. And now? Whoa, baby!

"Never a dull moment with you, even now. I came to see how you guys were doing. I know you and Sally were both pretty upset this morning," he explained. "Why are you doing the painting? I thought you would have hired someone."

"Hard times, my friend. Plus, we had the paint sitting around, so I figured why not get started," I answered with a shrug.

"If you want, I have some free time tomorrow. I could come back and help finish this."

"Aren't you busy out there catching criminals?"

"I'm off, and besides, things are at a standstill with my case right now.".

"If you wouldn't mind, that would be great." Plus, it would give me a chance to pick his brain and see what I could learn about the investigation regarding Morgan. "Tomorrow, it is."

"See you then."

CHAPTER FOURTEEN

I entered the building the next morning to find Chelsea loitering outside my office.

"Did we have a meeting today?" I asked.

She smiled. "Nooooo. I have something I need to run by you, though."

"Give me a minute to get settled," I said, passing by her so I get through the door and set my things down on my desk.

She followed close behind and plopped down in one of the client chairs. I put everything away and took a seat.

"Ready?" she sat up straight, a huge grin across her face."

I knew she had a hidden agenda. "What's up?"

"How would you like to go to dinner with Alex and me tonight?"

He was her newest guy. They came, they went. I seldom had the opportunity to meet them, let alone know them by name. There must be something special about this one.

"So, I can be a third wheel? No thanks," I responded, shaking my head.

"You wouldn't be the odd one out..." Chelsea's voice faded away, and the next part just sounded like mumbling.

My eyes narrowed. "What did you say?"

"Alex is bringing along a friend," she answered.

"A blind date? Even worse!" I exclaimed, rolling my eyes.

"Pretty please?" she pleaded, holding her hands up in a praying position.

I groaned. "No. I said no."

"Oh c'mon. You know you could use some fun in your life. Let your hair down a little."

"I'm honestly not in the mood." How could she even suggest it after all the stuff that's happened over the last few days?

"Leah, jeez. I'm not telling you to marry the guy. Just come out and have some dinner. Who knows, you might enjoy yourself. Crazy concept," Chelsea pestered, twirling her right pointer finger around the side of her head.

I let out a deep sigh. "I know, I know."

"Besides, you owe me."

"I do? How so?" I raised my eyebrow.

"Three things. High School. Lincoln Adams. First kiss."

Oh, my God. She wanted me to go bad if she brought that up. Peter Demonico held *the* party of the year, and somehow, I scored an invitation. My nerves bothered me so much, I begged Chelsea to give me a mini makeover so I would look cool. Everyone ended up playing a game of spin the bottle, and I had my initial smooch with Lincoln Adams.

"Jeez, that happened years ago, and it was the worst kiss ever." I shuddered, remembering Lincoln's slimy tongue shoved down my throat.

"True," she laughed. "Let's make a deal. Just come, and if you feel uncomfortable or you're not enjoying yourself, you can leave."

"Fine." I pointed at her. "I'll hold you to that."

"Yay! I knew I would wear you down!" My best friend jumped up and did a victory dance in front of my desk.

I gave her a dirty look as a resigned feeling of dread settled into the pit of my stomach.

"Now go. Shoo. I've got stuff to do." I waved my hands towards her.

"Make sure you put on something cute. No yoga pants!" she said as she strolled out of the office.

Damn, she knew me too well.

"Noted!" I yelled out.

She stuck her head back in. "And a little makeup wouldn't hurt either!"

I pointed to the door. "GO!"

The rest of the morning came and went. Things were quite sluggish. Luke phoned earlier, and we set a time for him to come over in the afternoon to finish painting. Chelsea and Meg had their own plans, so I hit up Caleb to see if he had anything going on.

"Hey, what's up?" I asked.

"Not much. Just finishing up some background checks for a client."

"Got any other plans?"

"Didn't I bring it up the other day? I secured an appointment to talk to Preston Coleman."

"No, you forgot to mention it. Can I tag along?"

"I believe it wouldn't be a good idea for him to see you. No offense," Caleb explained.

"None taken. How about I make you a deal? You meet with him, and I'll sneak into Morgan's office and do a little snooping?"

"I appreciate how you think, Jordan. Are you sure you're up for it? A company of that nature has its fair share of security equipment. You'll need to be ready to split if things get too hot. I won't be able to come to your aid. Please, be careful."

"When are you going to learn, Hamilton? I'll be fine. Trust me."

"Okay, okay. I can be there at two fifteen to pick you up. Is that enough time?"

"Perfect."

After we hung up, I remembered Luke would be coming back, and I had wanted to talk to him. That would have to have to wait. Hopefully, he would understand. An opportunity to explore Coleman Industries, I couldn't pass up.

Caleb and I arrived at the building and found a spot in the visitor's parking. Once we got inside, it felt like we entered a fancy four-star hotel, not a corporate office. The walls were gray marble, and an enormous crystal chandelier hung from the ceiling in the center. There were a couple of modern couches and numerous white leather high-backed chairs. Several magnificent pieces of artwork adorned the room, and a massive cherry desk with a receptionist waited at the rear near the two banks of elevators.

He signed us into the guest log and got our visitor passes. Preston's office was located on the third floor. We took the elevator up and stepped out into an enchanting, yet much darker, lobby. A lone administrative assistant sat there like a guard between two hallways that branched out to the left and right.

"Good afternoon, we're here to see Preston Coleman," he informed the employee.

"Do you have a scheduled meeting?" she asked, staring down her pointy nose at us.

"Yes, at two forty-five. I'm Caleb Hamilton of Hamilton and Associates," he answered.

"Let me check." She tapped her fingers on her keyboard for a couple of moments and glanced up, confirming it with a nod. "If you take a seat, I will inform him that you're here."

We stepped away and settled into a couple of chairs in the waiting area. She didn't leave to notify him like I expected. Maybe she sent him a text. Unfortunately, that wouldn't get her out of my snooping way. I began thinking of ways to get around the snooty receptionist. Maybe I could faint, fake a heart attack, or even a seizure? Aunt Sissy always said I had a flare for the dramatics. Before I could decide on the best way to flail and seize, a very upset man burst into the lobby from the elevators. He appeared extremely distressed. I held off on my performance and sat back to watch.

He looked around, breathing like an angry bull. "Where...is...he? I know he's here, that low-down scumbag has been sleeping with my wife!"

"Sir, please, you need to lower your voice. This is a place of business."

The receptionist stood up with only the desk between her and the enraged man. He ranted and talked so fast I couldn't make some of it out. However, if his temple veins bulged anymore, his head might explode all over the lobby.

"You inform that wife-stealing gigolo Randy Henderson, that I demand to see him IMMEDIATELY!"

"I'm afraid they're in a meeting. If you'll quiet down and have a seat, I can check if he'll come out once he's available."

Apparently, the man had enough. He charged around the left side of the receptionist's desk and down the hallway. Dumbfounded, she stood frozen in place with her mouth hanging open. She fumbled to grab her phone.

"Security, I need you now! Hurry, someone has breached the executive lobby on the third floor!" she exclaimed.

She slammed the receiver down and took off after him. I waited a few seconds to make sure she wasn't coming back and sneaked down to the other hall. If anyone stopped me, I would just pretend to be searching for the restroom. Cherry doors flanked both sides of the long passage. New and old pictures of Body by Mimi's products and ad campaigns lined the walls. I continued down the corridor, looking for Morgan's office.

Muffled sounds of people talking filled my ears from the direction of the disturbance. Trying not to draw attention to myself, I glanced around to make sure I didn't see anyone, especially the deranged individual. After a few minutes, I heard nothing. Either the soundproofing in the building was top-notch or the person had been subdued. Ahead of me were a pair of double doors with a keypad entry. Crap! I could be out of luck. I passed four more offices and nada. I started to turn around when one of them opened.

"Are you lost?" a well-dressed guy asked, coming towards me through the doorway.

"Oh gosh. I guess I am. They instructed me to head to the marketing department. Have I gone the wrong way?"

He gazed at me. "Are you new here? I don't believe I've seen you before."

"Is it that obvious?" I laughed and avoided looking him in the face as I tried to appear shy and clueless. My heart raced inside me, consumed by fear that the slightest eye contact would reveal my dishonesty.

"No need to worry. This place is a maze. I remember my first day. I'm Heath." He reached out to shake my hand.

"Olivia. Nice to meet you," I replied as we shook hands. Olivia? Where did that come from? Who cared if he didn't question it?

"Welcome to the company. Marketing offices are just through the door-ways on your right. Sorry, I would offer to show you, but I am running late for a conference call. See you around. Nice meeting you," Heath smiled as he held the entrance open so I could pass by.

"Thanks, you too," I called out. Three doors later, I found the one I searched for. Surveying my surroundings, I made sure the hallway remained clear before I turned the knob.

The door opened without issue. I closed it behind me. Morgan's decorating tastes carried over to his office. His desk served as the main focal point of the room. A big planner, computer monitor, keyboard, name placard, and some miscellaneous papers covered the surface. Bookshelves stood along each wall on either side.

I took a seat and pulled the calendar closer to me. Meetings and lunches filled most of the squares. I raised it to check for anything hidden underneath, and an envelope fell into my lap.

The sender addressed it to Morgan's home but didn't put any return information. Since the top was already open, I slid the note out and unfolded it. 'This must stop. Enclosed is the last money I will be sending'.

Who was giving Morgan money and why? I pulled my cell phone out and snapped a few pictures to show Caleb. Returning it to the envelope, I placed it back in its original location.

Crossing the room to the bookshelves, I scanned the shelves. Most of the books were self-help or business-related. When I got down to the third shelf, a hardback copy of Catcher in the Rye sat plain as day in between one on 'Marketing Strategies for the Twenty-First Century' and 'Sales Fundamentals for Dummies'. I stooped down and picked it up.

The weight of it didn't feel quite right. It was a fake designed to look like a book. I turned it on its side and lifted the top. Several newspaper clippings rested inside. As I tried to pull them out, a loud noise sounded in the hallway. Startled, I dropped the box, and the contents flew all over the place. I gathered everything up, shoved them in my bag and put the novel back on the shelf.

I hurried across the room and stood to listen at the door. I heard two male voices talking. A few minutes later, their conversation faded. I peeked out and glanced to the left and right. Nothing. I crept into the hall and shut the office door behind me.

To my surprise, I didn't come across anyone else and made it back to the executive lobby without incident. Neither the receptionist nor my partner were present, so I continued to the elevators. Once I reached the main entrance, I walked to the parking lot to find Caleb.

"Finally! I texted you. Didn't you get my message?" he asked as he stood by his car.

"Sorry. I lost track of time. I figured you were still talking to Mr. Coleman," I responded, opening the front passenger door.

My partner slid into the driver's seat.

"The man kept things brief and seemed to be in a hurry. He claimed Morgan was an outstanding employee and a great son-in-law-to-be. He didn't know anyone who may have wanted to cause harm to him. He just wants me to figure out who's responsible."

"That's it?"

"Yup. I couldn't get a solid read on him, and that never happens. There is still something I can't put my finger on. I wouldn't scratch him off the suspect list just yet. How did you do?"

"Pretty good. I found a picture, and some news clippings in a hidden box. Figure there might be something worthwhile in there."

"Great. Let's take them back to my office." Caleb replied.

"I wish I could. But I need to get home and prepare for tonight. How about we meet up tomorrow?"

"You're going to make me wait? Not like you have a hot date or anything, Jordan." He began laughing and turned to look at me. He stopped when he realized I wasn't joining him.

"Uh... actually, I do," I replied.

Caleb's cheeks grew red. "I didn't mean to imply that you couldn't have one..."

I cut him off. "It's fine, Hamilton. Not a big deal. Chelsea called in a favor. I'm just obliging."

We filled the rest of our ride with small talk and awkward silence.

My best friend and her boyfriend Alex were going to pick me up in twenty minutes, and still had no clue what to wear. The girls were no help when I asked their opinion. They just rolled all over the things I'd laid out on the bed.

A few minutes later, I stood in front of the bathroom mirror and gave myself one last look over. Casual, but not too casual. I selected a silky floral tank top, layered under a mauve half sweater, and paired it with blue jeans and my favorite brown boots. A simple silver necklace completed my outfit.

Opening the drawer to the left of the sink, I plucked out tubes of lip gloss and mascara, applied a light layer of each and called it done. I picked up my purse, said goodbye to the cats and walked out to the porch. Perfect timing, because Chelsea had just pulled into my driveway.

She spared no expense in many facets of her life, cars included. An absolutely gorgeous 2016, silver BMW 3 Series rolled to a stop in front of me. Her date, Alex, exited from the passenger's side and opened my door. He stood six-foot-three, with long blonde hair, and blue eyes, and had a slender but muscular build. He fit her type to a tee.

"You look great! I love the tank," my bestie called out as she leaned over to greet me.

"Thanks," I said as I slid into the backseat. My stomach was doing flip-flops in anticipation. On the one hand, I knew I needed to put myself out there again, on the other, I didn't want to have my heart broken again.

Alex closed it and got back inside the car. I expected my date would be waiting in the rear, but he wasn't.

Chelsea noticed the confused look on my face. "Don't worry, he didn't bail. His friend is meeting us at the restaurant. He's finishing some last-minute stuff up at work. This is Alex, by the way."

"Nice to meet you, Leah. Chelsea's told me a lot about you," he said as he turned around to shake my hand.

We shook. "Same to you," I replied.

The happy couple filled the rest of the drive with nonstop chatting. I kept to myself, replaying everything we knew about Morgan's murder and tuned them out. After talking to the people we had interviewed thus far, there were a few potential suspects but not one that set off bells and whistles yet. Then coming across the different identities and bank accounts with deposited large amounts of money, my intuition told me we didn't know Morgan at all.

Learning Janie's ex came back in the picture opened a new can of worms. Could he have wanted her enough to get her fiancé out of the way? Before I knew it, we'd arrived at Stella's, and Alex had opened my door for me.

"Thanks, you didn't need to do that," I expressed, stepping out of the car.

"It is my pleasure," he replied.

We entered the restaurant, and the hostess led us to a beautiful table in the middle of the room. It was decorated with a trio of differing-sized crystal vases with floating candles on top of a crisp white linen tablecloth, and the chairs were high-backed leather. She handed each person in our group a menu, and we perused them. The server came to take our drink orders and brought out a loaf of sourdough bread and herbed butter.

"I see you're waiting for one more. Would you like to order an appetizer?" she asked.

Chelsea spoke up. "We'll wait, thank you."

I lifted my glass of ice water and sipped. Everything looked so delicious, I couldn't decide. After battling my taste buds, I decided on a side salad with a raspberry vinegarette dressing and chicken marsala as my entrée. I pilfered a slice of bread from the basket, tore it in half and spread on some butter.

"About time, man! What took you so long?" Alex exclaimed just as I devoured a bite.

"Sorry, I got held up at the station. Paperwork," his friend replied.

Shock washed over me, and I choked on my bite of bread. I knew that voice.

Chelsea jumped up next to me, slapping my back. "Leah, are you okay?"

I turned around and came face to face with Luke Strickland.

CHAPTER FIFTEEN

"Y-y-you? You're my date?" I got out after I coughed my head off.

"Wait. Do you two know each other?" Chelsea's partner asked, looking back and forth between Luke and me.

He nodded. "We all grew up together. They're best friends with my sister Meg."

"Wow! Small world," Alex exclaimed.

I glanced over at my best friend and mouthed the words, 'Were you aware of this?'.

She shook her head no.

"How do you guys know one another?" I asked.

"Sherlock... I mean Luke and I play on an intramural basketball team over at the rec center," Alex explained. "It's been what, four or five years now?"

"Give or take," he answered as he took a seat next to me.

A bemused grin tugged at my lips. "Sherlock?"

He blushed and sighed. "Yeah, we all have nicknames."

Chelsea nudged Alex's side. "What's yours?"

Before he could answer, the server returned to take our orders. We chose an Antipasto platter for the table as an appetizer and requested more time to select our main courses. An awkward silence fell over the table. It drove me crazy. I figured I should make the best of it.

"You got interrupted before. What were you going to say? I queried.

"Oh, yes, where was I? My name. That's right. The guys all call me 'Count' because I work with numbers. You know from *Sesame Street*," my friend's date responded.

We all chuckled.

"That's cute. So, Alex, tell me more about yourself. What do you do for a living?" I asked.

"I work for Halston and Bunch LLC, an accounting firm in Columbus."

"Nice. How did you two get together?"

"We met at an awful mixer held by a local networking group. We bonded over the crab rangoon appetizer, which was the only edible food."

She laughed. "Oh, my god. He's not kidding."

"A couple of glasses of wine, and we were talking like old friends." Alex smiled, placed his hand over Chelsea's, and gave it a little squeeze.

How sweet! I wouldn't believe it till I'd seen it, but so far, this guy seemed decent and different from the guys she'd dated in the past. Most of her previous ones, we'd either never met, or they turned out to be users and cheaters.

I glanced over at Luke. "Did everything turn out okay at The Wedded Bliss earlier? "I'm sorry I didn't make it back before you left," I asked.

"I think it looks much better. I'll let you be the ultimate judge, though," he replied.

I breathed a silent sigh of relief that he didn't get mad when I abandoned him, and I thanked him with sincerity. "We appreciate it."

"Anytime. Have any of you guys eaten here before? What's good?" Luke asked.

"I have. The Chicken Parmesan is delicious. Another excellent choice is the beef tenderloin filet," Alex suggested.

The server came back to take our orders and brought more bread with our salads. The conversation lulled as the men dug in like they hadn't eaten all day. My friend and I attacked our plates in a more civilized manner.

"We talked about Alex's profession. How are things at work, Luke?" Chelsea piped up after we'd had a few bites.

"Right now, pretty steady. I think I've seen the inside of the station more than my house these last couple of weeks," he answered.

"Any luck on finding a suspect in Morgan's murder?" she asked.

My old crush smiled and shook his head. "You know I can't talk about active cases. Let's just say we will not stop until we find the truth."

She shrugged her shoulders. "I had to ask. It's all anyone is talking about. Not something we're used to dealing with here in Ashford."

"Leah, Chelsea mentioned you inherited the business from your aunt?" Alex asked, changing the subject.

"Yes. We lost her a few months ago."

"I'm sorry to hear that."

"Thank you. Quite a woman in her own right. I just hope that I can continue the legacy she and my mother started. It helps that I have my two best friends to help me," I said, looking over at Chelsea with a smile.

She grinned. "We make a great team."

The rest of the evening remained enjoyable, with casual conversation, jokes, and delicious food. I am glad I decided to go out. I learned more about Alex and saw a new side of Luke. Until recent events it had been years since I'd seen Meg's brother. We'd both grown and matured.

It grew late, and Alex had an early meeting the next day, so we called it a night. The handsome detective offered me a ride to let my bestie drop her beau off and have a bit of alone time. We reached his truck in the parking lot. He opened the door for me and waited to make sure I got in.

I glanced over at him. "Thanks for taking me home. Hope it's not too much of an inconvenience."

"Not at all. I offered, remember?" he replied.

"Did you have a great time tonight?" I asked.

He nodded. "I did. How about you?"

I blushed. "It shocked me a little to see you were my date, but I'm glad it turned out to be you."

"Were you expecting an ogre or something?" he inquired, with a raised eyebrow.

I laughed. "No, but you know Chelsea. Her previous choices have been questionable, to say the least. Plus, she's pressuring me to put myself out there since things ended with my ex-fiancé."

"Touché. Remember the one she met at the heavy metal concert?"

"Yeah, he wasn't such a bad guy, though, just very different from who she usually dated. So, how did Alex convince you to come tonight?"

He sighed. "All the guys on the team have been on my case to get a girlfriend. They keep telling me I work too much and need some fun in my life. It's been so long since I've been in the dating scene, I'm kind of rusty."

"I know how you feel. Now, it's all about those dating sites and swiping left or swiping right."

"What happened to the old meeting someone at the store or out at a bar?" he chuckled.

"Who knows?" I replied with a shrug. "Seems like people just don't want to make any real effort anymore."

I had him alone, so I decided to see what he would tell me about Morgan's investigation. "You mentioned earlier you've been busy at the police department. Does that mean you're close to catching the killer?"

Luke cleared his throat. "Like I told Chelsea, you know I can't comment on an active case."

I nodded. "I get it. I do. Between the lawsuit and now the vandalism, I'm even more concerned about the future of The Wedded Bliss. I would hate it if we were to close, and the girls lost their jobs. Is there anything you could tell me to put my mind at ease?"

Luke glanced over at me, then back to the road. "If you repeat any of this, I will deny it. There are a couple of suspects we have at the top of our list. Before filing charges, we have a lot more witnesses to speak with. Plus, there's evidence that needs to be analyzed. I know it seems dire right now, but I just ask that you have faith in my team."

He turned down my street, and a few minutes later, we pulled into my driveway.

I shifted my gaze towards Luke. "Thanks again for tonight and bringing me home. For what it's worth, listen to your friends. Any girl would be lucky to have you, and you deserve some fun in your life."

Teenage Leah would be freaking out right now, sitting in a car with her biggest crush. I didn't know if I should give him a warm embrace or shake his hand. I felt so awkward but attempted a side hug. As I moved closer to him, my purse strap got caught up in my door handle and I ended up falling into him. Built very solid, he smelled very fresh and clean. He grasped my arm to steady me. Frozen, I attempted to play it cool and leaned back in my seat.

My face heated up and I stared down at my feet. "I am so sorry. You must think I am the biggest idiot."

Luke placed his hand under my chin, bringing my head up and looking me in the eye. "Leah, there are many thoughts I have about you, and idiot is not one of them."

Whoa.

I laughed nervously and felt the need to escape before my clumsy self did anything else embarrassing. "Thanks. I better get going. The kitties are in there wasting away. Have a good night."

"You too," he replied.

He waited till I got my door unlocked and stepped in before he backed out of the driveway.

The last few days ran together. I had been so busy with Caleb and the case. Overdue for some girl time, Meg, Chelsea, and I all planned to meet at Dottie's Diner. Around longer than I could remember, the old place was a true gem disguised as a hole in the wall with down-home cooking at low prices.

I walked in and the delectable aroma of bacon and pancakes flooded my nostrils. Neither of the girls had shown up yet, so I chose a booth in the back. I slid in on the right side, facing the front door, so I could flag them down when they arrived. Placing my coat and purse on the seat next to me, I ordered apple juice and ice water while I waited.

The server brought me a menu which I started perusing. My eyes scanned the pages, and I began playing a little game I called, 'How bad should I be?'. My stomach said to order the sausage gravy with biscuits, while my brain suggested ordering the turkey bacon with eggbeaters and fruit. Before I could decide, my girlfriends strolled in the front door. I waved them over.

"Glad you both made it," I said.

"Thanks. You weren't waiting too long, were you?" Meg asked.

"Nope. You guys just saved me from ordering a gazillion calories," I replied, placing my menu on the table.

Chelsea laughed. "Last night wasn't that bad now, right?"

The server returned with two more menus and took the girls' drink orders.

"No...but all this stress has me extra hungry." I muttered. "How are you, Meg?"

"Exhausted. Delaney is experiencing sleep regression, and if she doesn't start sleeping through the night, this mama is going to lose it."

"I'm tired too, but for a totally different reason, if you get my drift," Chelsea winked.

I groaned.

Meg grimaced and shook her head. "TMI! What about you, Leah?"

"Work, eat, sleep, repeat. With some investigating thrown in."

"That's all that's going on, eh?" She gave me a knowing look.

I blushed. "Chels already told you about last night, huh? I had a nice time."

"Nice? Just nice?" Meg stared at me.

"Well, a little awkward at first, but I ended up enjoying myself. He's not the same guy I remembered," I answered.

Chelsea waggled her eyebrows. "Does that mean you *like* him?"

"One date, jeez! I do not believe I am the best person to be entering into a new relationship right now, no matter who it's with. Plus, he's Meg's brother. Wouldn't that be kind of weird?"

"Maybe, but don't write it off. Sometimes, the most effective way to get over someone is to meet someone new. Caleb's not too bad on the eyes either. Just saying."

"Oh yeah, Caleb is h-o-t, hot. I wouldn't have a problem if you dated Luke, though. But if you hurt him, you'll have to answer to me." Meg made a face, trying to look tough and threatening.

I sighed. "Oy. Enough about my love life or lack thereof. I need to pick your brains about the case."

"What's going on?" Meg asked.

"We have been able to talk to several people, but I'm not sure we're any closer than when we started."

"Anyone you've managed to eliminate?" Chelsea asked.

I shrugged. "Sort of. Janie is the closest to him, but I can't see her or her bridesmaids killing someone. God forbid, they break a sweat or a nail."

That made both of my friends giggle.

Chelsea cleared her throat. "We shouldn't be laughing, but that's funny."

"Has Luke mentioned anything to you about the case?" I asked, looking at his sister.

"I wish. He stays tight-lipped and brooding when he's got an investigation. It's like when we were kids, and he had a secret. Not even our mom could get him to crack," she replied.

Chelsea wondered, "Have you heard any more about..."

Before she could finish her sentence, the server came back to take our orders and bring the girls their drinks. The evil side of my conscience won out, and I went with the sausage gravy and biscuits.

"What were you going to ask?" I prompted.

"I just wanted to know if you heard anything about who vandalized The Wedded Bliss?"

"No, not yet. I reached out to the police department earlier, but they haven't found any evidence that connects to a suspect."

"I hope they figure it out soon," Meg commented.

By that time, our food came, and we all attacked our plates like ravenous animals. We spent the next hour having a relaxed conversation before we all went our separate ways.

CHAPTER SIXTEEN

"Are you certain you're comfortable with going back to Morgan's condo?" he asked me later that day.

"I'll be fine. Plus, I brought my pepper spray with me this time," I replied.

He sighed. "That may dissuade someone, but it won't halt them."

"Let's just go," I said, giving him a look.

Caleb took off, and we made it to the apartment. It looked different in the daylight than I remembered. He pulled the car around to the alley between our victim's street and the next one over. We parked a few places past it and walked back.

Huge green metal dumpsters sat three to four yards apart. We reached the one closest to Morgan's. A heavy black plastic lid split in half covered it. I opened the one on the right slightly, stood on my tippy toes and peered in. The garbage container was stacked to the brim with trash. The stench emanating from inside assaulted my nostrils.

"Oh, man. Who came up with this idea again?" I asked, pinching my nose shut and looking back at Caleb

"I got word that people witnessed someone cleaning out Morgan's apartment, so I thought we'd scope out the dumpsters. Not the most glamorous part of my job, but one man's trash can provide a treasure of information," he responded with a grin.

"I'll believe that when I see it," I muttered under my breath.

"Oh, c'mon, Jordan. A little dirt never hurt anybody."

"That's not what I'm worried about. It's all the other stuff people may have tossed in there."

"Touché. Let's get started. I'll help you climb in and then join you. Here, take these and put them on."

Caleb handed me a pair of gloves. He didn't have to tell me twice. I pulled them on as high as they would go without tearing the latex. As soon as I got inside, the smell became a gazillion times worse. It took all my willpower to keep the bile from rising in my throat. I grasped my first bag, ripped a hole in it, and began sifting through the awful contents. It contained lots of kitchen and food waste but no identifying items. I put it to the side and moved onto the next.

We had both gone through about five bags each and kept striking out.

"How many more should we search?" I wondered.

"Let's give it a little more time. This dumpster is quite full," Caleb responded.

The longer I hunted the more discouraged I became that we wouldn't find anything. Plus, I had no idea what to look for. The further down we dug, the harder it got to pull them from the bottom. The ones on top were falling back over in my work area. I attempted to lift my left foot, and it stuck to the sludge beneath.

"I think I stumbled upon something!" he whispered loudly.

Oh, thank gosh!" I turned around to check it out. "Whatcha got?"

"I think I've discovered some items addressed to him."

I waded over to Caleb, and he handed me a few pieces of mail.

"Great. Is there anything else that might be worth taking?" I inquired.

"Let me see," he reached back down into the bag. "Doesn't seem like it."

A loud truck rumbled nearby. It sounded familiar, but I couldn't quite place it. I peeked out over the top of the dumpster. A massive green and white waste disposal vehicle barreled towards us down the alley. Oh crap!

"Caleb, we need to go...now!" I yelled.

"What?" my partner called back as he bent over to continue checking bags.

"The garbage truck is here!" I exclaimed. "If we don't leave immediately, we'll end up smushed in here!"

He stood up straight and realized I wasn't joking. "Here, you hold on to this stuff while I lift you up. Then I'll follow."

I took the mail from his hand and clutched it tight to my chest as he boosted me up. Once I hit the ground, I noticed the vehicle was only a few feet away.

"Hurry, it's getting closer!"

He jumped up and swung his leg over the side. After he clambered out, we booked it. Our pumping adrenaline lent us speed, but we still huffed like freight trains when we reached the car.

"What a close call," I gasped.

He let out a deep breath and shook his head. "Can you imagine if we didn't get out of there?"

"'Death by dumpster' is not a headline I'd want to read."

I glanced over at Caleb and noticed he had a strange look on his face.

I ran my hands over my face. "What? Do I have something on me?"

"No. Just come closer."

I moved towards him, and he reached out, plucking an object from my head.

"You had a little worm in your hair," he explained, holding out his hand.

"A what? Ew!" I shrieked. "Are there any more? Get them off!"

"Don't worry, the only thing it will do is give someone a sugar rush. See?" he chuckled.

He placed it in my right hand. It was part of a gummy worm.

I groaned and tossed it back at him. "You are so frustrating."

He burst out laughing as it bounced off his forehead. "Sorry, I couldn't help myself, Jordan. Just too funny. You should have seen your face."

"Hmph! See if I participate in dumpster diving again with you!"

"Ready to go? I don't know about you, but I reek, and I'd like to get cleaned up before I do anything else."

I agreed. "Sounds good."

Caleb dropped me off at home and said once he got showered and changed, he would meet me back at my house.

An hour later, after one hot shower, lots of scrubbing and two rounds of shampoo and conditioner, I felt like a new woman. I went to the kitchen to prepare some finger food but discovered my options were severely limited. I badly needed to make a trip to the store. Scrounging up a box of Triscuits, I sliced up some Colby jack cheese and arranged everything on a plate.

Caleb showed up, and we got settled across from each other at the table. We both took out our notes.

"Why don't we start by reviewing the facts we've collected so far, then we can discuss our suspects and where we go from here?" he suggested.

"I agree. We know that Morgan Vanderbilt died by stabbing. It occurred sometime between 8:30 p.m. and 9:30 p.m. on Friday. He worked as an employee at Coleman Industries, which is owned by his fiancée's father. No one hated him, but they didn't like him much either.," I summarized.

"Let's review our suspect pool," he said. "Janie and her bridesmaids have been cleared. They all have solid alibis. When Morgan died, several of the guests observed them on the dance floor."

"I don't really see her having the means to do it. She is too occupied with climbing the social ladder and keeping up her image. Killing someone would not look good for a socialite. As for the bridesmaids, none of them had a reason to want to harm Morgan." I replied.

"From my perspective, the groomsmen can be marked off, too."

"Chelsea didn't and wouldn't do it as the police found out," I stated. "I never doubted her from the start. Who does that leave?" I flipped to the next page in my notepad. "The Coleman's, Dalton McVay, Theodore Banks, and Marcus Deaver."

"Just an instance of in the wrong place at the wrong time at the bar. Anytime alcohol is involved, it never ends well." Caleb commented.

"We should consider following up with her ex-fiancé and see what he has to say for himself. Very convenient he would show up now," I murmured.

"That just leaves the bride's parents. Her mother never hid the fact she didn't care for Morgan."

I made a huge circle around their names. "No love lost there. Her father's a little harder to read."

"I think it's time for another talk with him. Don't you agree?" Caleb asked.

"Great idea. Did you bring the mail we found in the trash?"

"Yes, let me grab it," Caleb said as he reached down to open his briefcase. "I didn't look at all of it yet."

He laid the envelopes on the table in between us.

I plucked the top one from the pile and unfolded the letter. "Appears to be a bill of some sort." I skimmed the page. "Morgan ordered some suits from a company called Marshtons."

He examined the piece he picked up. "This is a bank statement. However, there's something odd. It's a shared account, and the other name on it is Jason Eakins. Why does that sound familiar?"

I perked up. "Jason Eakins? That's the exact one I came across on items at Morgan's desk at his apartment.

"You're right! Another interesting thing, there are some very large deposits in this account. Body by Mimi is thriving, and while executive positions pay well, the generous amounts I'm seeing are unusual."

"I located one similar at his condo, and it also showed several huge sums. I wrote them down. How much are those?" I asked.

"The first on this statement occurred May 2nd, in the amount of $25,000. Two weeks later, there is another entry for an additional $25,000."

"Holy moly! That is a great deal of moolah. I agree it can't be from his job, so where does it come from? Let me retrieve my notes." I flipped to the page where I had copied the information. "One April 10th, a deposit of $20,000, and another on the 24th. When we met about planning the wedding, it didn't seem like Morgan could contribute much. Even to the rehearsal dinner, which is traditionally the groom or groom's family's responsibility," I explained.

"There are only a few reasons individuals receive that amount of money in a short period of time. Either they came into a huge inheritance, they won the lottery, or someone is trying to buy their silence." Caleb said.

"Who would want Morgan to be quiet, and what did he need to be quiet about?" I wondered.

"Those would be the million-dollar questions. The first thing we need to do is find out as much as we can about Jason Eakins. The name has shown up twice now among Morgan's belongings. Let's go back through all our notes and see if there is anything we may have missed or overlooked regarding what we have learned about our victim. Anything that could seem out of place."

"Sounds good. We should also compile a list from the witnesses and suspects we have that would have the means to pay off someone." Before I could finish the rest of my thought, my cell phone rang. I picked it up from the table and pressed the answer button.

"Hello?"

"Leah, are you coming in today?" Meg asked.

"I should be there soon. Is everything okay?"

"It is. Chef Stefan mentioned one of our servers needed to talk to you, regarding something, he witnessed the night of the rehearsal dinner."

"He's there now?" I clarified.

"Yes," she replied.

"Let me finish up here, and I will be there soon."

"See you then."

Caleb glanced at me. "Need to go?"

I closed my notebook and shoved it into my bag. "Yeah. Meg told me one of our servers has some information about something he saw the night of the rehearsal dinner. Is it possible for us to catch up later?"

"Sure. I think we got a lot figured out. It will give me time to investigate further into Janie's ex-fiancé. It might be good to try to determine what he's been up to since he came back to town."

"Perfect. I'll also follow up with Ted Banks and see if there is anything we may have missed."

Caleb and I gathered up our notes and got ready to leave. I did a quick review of the cats' food and water bowls and topped them off. The girls just looked at me from their perches and went back to sleep. I felt a pang of jealousy at the stress-free lives they were forced to lead.

I'd just walked in and taken a seat when I heard, "Ms. Jordan?"

I glanced up from my desk and found Devin, one of our longtime servers, standing at my office door.

His sweet temper and reliability made him a great employee, and his tall, lanky build lent him an adorable air of awkwardness, especially because he wore his bangs a bit long and always had to brush them out of his eyes. In college now, he still made himself available for big events and weekends.

"Are *you* the person Meg told me about?" I verified. "What's up? Come in and make yourself comfortable."

He shuffled in and took one of the client chairs across from me. He laced his hands together and dropped them in his lap. "Chef Stefan thought I should pay you a visit."

"Everything all right?" I asked.

"Yes—no. I'm not sure. I witnessed something the night of the Coleman event. I originally brushed it off. After what happened, I figured someone should know what I observed," he explained.

"Let me shut my door, and you can tell me what you saw." I crossed the room to do just that and returned to my desk.

I wanted to ensure that no one interrupted us. I got my notebook out of my bag and turned to a blank page in order to record every detail. Even the smallest thing could lead to a break in the case.

"Devin, why don't you start from the beginning? You said this occurred the night of the Coleman-Vanderbilt rehearsal dinner. About what time would you say?" I asked.

"Let me think. Dessert had been served around 8 P.M. It occurred after that I'd say. We were cleaning up and starting to take out the first round of trash to the dumpster." he explained.

I nodded. "Go on."

"When I went out back, a vehicle I didn't recognize sat behind the building."

"What type was it? Can you remember?" I asked.

"A black, four-door sedan. Not sure of the make."

"Could you make out a license plate?"

"No, sorry. I only caught a glimpse of it. I saw a dent or scrape on the rear driver-side panel."

I wrote down every word he said. "Why are you just bringing it up now?

"We were so busy that night, then everything happened. It kept bothering me that maybe there was some importance to it, and I should speak up. I felt scared going to the police, so that's why I came to you."

"I appreciate you coming forward. I'll be sure that someone looks into it. If you remember anything more you let me know."

He stood up and started to leave but paused and turned around. "Wait. I recall something else."

I looked back up at him. "Okay."

"On the rear above the back tire and near the dent, a partially scraped-off vinyl tag or bumper sticker was visible," he mentioned.

"What did it resemble? Can you try and describe it?"

"It was rounded on the sides and almost a half-circle at the bottom, but the top part was missing."

I began a rough sketch as he talked. My artistic ability lacked finesse, but once I finished, I realized it looked familiar to me.

"Is this close?" I turned my notepad around to show Devin my drawing.

"Kind of. There were lines going vertical from the bottom towards the top of the half circle," he explained.

I continued adding details until he felt it looked accurate to what he remembered.

I thanked him for the second time. After he left my office, I turned on my computer and wore out my eyes for an hour searching the internet for something resembling the emblem or logo he'd described. I gave up when my vision grew blurry and decided to try again later.

CHAPTER SEVENTEEN

I couldn't put my heart and soul into The Wedded Bliss if my mind was preoccupied. We must have missed something. I planned to go over my notes from the investigation. Before I could get started, Meg appeared at my office door.

"Hey, you okay, Leah? "she inquired.

I closed my notebook. "Yeah, merely overthinking."

"I just wanted to touch base with you. It seems lately like we're passing ships in the night."

"I'm sorry. I know I haven't been around as often."

"It's okay. We're making progress on whittling down the delinquent accounts. Between Chelsea and I, we've managed to reach out to over half the clients with outstanding amounts and started collecting from them. Others we have been able to set up payment plans, and the rest we still need to follow up with."

"Wow, that's great! Thank you so much for all your hard work."

She gave me a smile. "Of course. We are a team, a family. We're not going down without a fight. Chelsea can fill you in later about the specific progress, but we're making headway.

"Have we heard from Allison and Conner yet?" I asked.

"We have. They did decide to go with The Wedded Bliss."

I let out a long sigh. Oh, thank God. "Awesome! I was starting to worry."

"It's a ray of hope. Stay positive, woman," my friend chided me. "How is the investigation going? Luke still won't tell me much except they've got 'all available resources working on it' and they're 'getting closer' to arresting a suspect."

"I think pretty good. It feels like we're so close, yet so far away," I lamented.

"If anyone can figure this out, it's you. You've always had a knack for solving problems."

"I hope you're right."

Meg left, and I brought out the news clippings and papers I found in the secret book at Morgan's office. I spread them out in front of me on my desk. The initial piece listed a date from 2008. The headline of the article read 'Local company launches new product line'. I scanned the caption at the bottom. 'From L to R, Stuart Rodgers, Willis Haskell, Preston Coleman, Mitch Eakins'.

They all stood behind a counter display with an assortment of bath products for men. Mr. Coleman looked the same. The thing that caught my attention was the final person, Mitch Eakins. He had to be some relation to Morgan, er, Jason, whatever his name was. Eakins wasn't a typical surname, especially around here.

I flipped through more of the papers and found a specific one that appeared to be a report containing some kind of lab results. There were a bunch of words that sounded super complicated: phenoxyethanol something, along with lanolin, herbal extracts, and red dye. The ingredient water was circled. I would have to do some further research to figure out what they tested.

That evening, I stood in the shower, letting the warm water cascade over me. Picking up the shampoo, I began lathering my hair. The more I massaged my head and worked it in, the more relaxed I became. Then it hit me like a ton of bricks.

I recognized the decal on the car that Devin tried to describe! I turned to face the shower doors and used my finger to draw in the steam. As I completed the drawing, I realized the half-circle was the bottom of a lotus blossom.

The flowers were part of the Body by Mimi's logo. I saw them all over the office building the day I went with Caleb. Sliding open the door, I plucked a towel off the rack and jumped out of the shower. My left foot caught on the edge of the tub, which caused me to stumble. My arms flailed for balance as I reached out to steady myself.

My big toe hurt something awful. I half hopped and half limped down the hall to my bedroom. I sat on the bed and put my laptop on the night-stand. It only took a minute to bring up the company's website. When it loaded, a huge lotus flower appeared in the left corner of the web page.

In the middle up near the top of the banner, a slide show played. As the pictures scrolled by, one caught my eye. Preston Coleman, CEO, stood with the current COO and CFO in front of the Body by Mimi building headquarters. I clicked the photo to enlarge it. A fleet of black sedans was visible in the parking lot in the background. Sure enough, on the rear panel of the closest car, the lotus logo could be observed.

I had to call Caleb! Picking my cellphone up, I scrolled to his number in my contact list and hit send.

"Jordan. What's up?" he answered.

"You won't believe what I just found out. I know who owns the vehicle that Devin saw that night at The Wedded Bliss. It's a Body by Mimi company car." I babbled so fast I wasn't sure if Caleb understood me.

After what felt like forever, he let out a deep breath and spoke. "Wait, what? How did you figure it out? Are you positive?"

"Funniest thing, as I stood in the shower..." I explained.

"Oh, really now?" his husky voice drawled.

My face warmed, and I self-consciously tugged the towel up even though he couldn't see me. "Focus! Anyway, I kept thinking about the decal and my rough drawing of it. That's when it hit me. It's the lotus flower symbol from the Body by Mimi's logo!"

"You have got to be kidding me," he gasped.

"Now we have to locate the car, correct?" I questioned.

"Yes, and we need to figure out who drove it that night," Caleb replied.

"Isn't it obvious?" I exclaimed.

"Jordan, many people could have access to those vehicles. "

"True, but I believe we shouldn't wait."

"If the killer was behind the wheel of that vehicle, they're dangerous. I believe it would be a good idea to loop Strickland in on this."

"What if that takes too long? He could flee." I grumbled.

"Let me reach out to him. Don't take any action until you hear from me," Caleb directed.

I let out an exasperated sigh. "Fine. I won't do anything."

"On another note, I've been looking into Janie's ex-fiancé. He works for an IT company in Columbus as a systems analyst. He owns a condo downtown and has lived there since 2013," Caleb explained.

"Were you able to talk to anyone who knows him?" I asked.

"Yes. I spoke with a few of his acquaintances, an old co-worker, and some neighbors. They described him as confident yet cocky. Smart, but he had a short temper and loved the nightlife a little too much. While the people I interviewed didn't say they hated him, I don't think any of them were his best friends," he responded.

"Has he had any run-ins with the law?" I wondered.

"Funny you should mention that. I found a few records. Appears our boy has a problem with alcohol. He's had two DUIs in the past five years."

"Did he do any jail time?"

"No. In the first case, he fought it and pled down to reckless operation of a vehicle. The second offense, they sentenced him to attend an intensive driving school," Caleb replied.

"And people wonder what is wrong with our justice system," I grumbled.

"That's a debate for a later time. But he's not who we're looking for."

"How can you be sure? He sounds unstable to me. Alcohol issues, cocky, short temper, and scorned lover? That sounds like a perfect recipe for a murderer."

"I reached out to a friend of mine at the Breckenridge County Sheriff's Office and turns out Dalton McVay was drying out in a cell. He got picked up for drunk and disorderly outside the bar at the Ashford Inn. Which means there's no way he was anywhere near The Wedded Bliss the night of the rehearsal," Caleb reported.

"So, it's possible that he came back to town to woo Janie, but his struggles with alcohol intervened?" I guessed.

"Sounds like it. When they picked him up, witnesses mentioned he went on and on about how he lost the love of his life. It appears that she rebuffed his attempt at reconciliation, and he went on a bender to drown his sorrows," he replied.

"Wow. I feel bad for the guy. Not because of his legal issues but breaking up or losing someone sucks no matter the circumstances," I murmured.

Caleb promised to call me back after talking to Luke. Meanwhile, I reached out to Ted Banks and set up another meeting later at the Fox and Hound.

I walked into the restaurant and noticed he had already arrived and had taken a booth to my right. As I approached, he stood up to greet me, and I sat down across from him.

"Good to see you, Mr. Banks. Thank you for agreeing to meet with me once again."

"Sure, no problem," he replied and returned to his seat.

"I have some more questions about Body by Mimi. Did you think of anyone else that might have had an issue with Morgan?" I started.

"No, I considered what we talked about last time. Maybe if he and I were closer, I could be of more help."

"What details can you share with me about the company cars?" I asked.

He began tapping his fingers together. "What do you want to know?"

I couldn't determine if my queries were irritating him, or if he wanted to avoid answering. "Who has access to the vehicles?"

"The executive-level employees," he answered.

I noted his answer and underlined it. That narrowed it down.

I glanced back up. "Have you ever used one?"

"A couple of times to travel to marketing conferences, etc. Not anytime recently, though. I'm not sure what this has to do with Morgan?" he sighed, looking down at his watch.

My continued questioning obviously irritated him.

I planned to tread lightly, but I needed more information. "Just humor me, please. How easy is it to use a company car?"

"I would say it's hard. There is a long approval process. A request has to be submitted in writing at least three weeks before the date or dates you need to use it. First, it gets sent to your direct manager, then the department head signs off and lastly, Preston Coleman gives the final say," Ted elaborated.

"Were there any constraints on when you could take one?" I inquired.

"They were only supposed to be signed out during the week. Unless you had to travel to a client or a conference over a certain distance. In the past, a couple of employees abused the privilege, and the insurance premium went up from what I heard," he explained.

"When was the last time you drove one?" I asked.

"I believe it would have been a few weeks ago. We had a meeting with our printing companies in Cincinnati," he answered.

"I also wanted to follow up with you since our previous conversation and see if there might be any new information or insight you have about the case.

"No, I told you pretty much everything I know," his body language told me otherwise. He crossed his arms and shifted his weight.

"Are you certain there's nothing else you have to tell me?" I wheedled.

Maybe my imagination caused me to think he lied, but something seemed off.

"It's probably not a big deal...," his voice trailed off as he continued to fidget.

"Could you explain what you mean, please? Even the smallest detail could be important," I used the calm coaxing voice I employed when diffusing a bridezilla tantrum.

"The night of the rehearsal dinner, I told you I stayed in the banquet room the whole time. That's not true. At one point in the evening, I stepped out to make a telephone call. That's when I heard people arguing," he confessed.

He definitely had my undivided attention. "Go on."

"I couldn't make out what they said, but I figured it was a result of the stress from the wedding. I finished my conversation and went back in."

"You weren't able to see them?"

"Not from where I stood, but I recognized one of the voices as Preston Coleman's." He chewed on his lower lip.

You could have knocked me over with a feather. I sure didn't expect him to say Preston Coleman. Either he was mistaken, or the bride's father was one heck of an actor. His reaction the night of the rehearsal, the lawsuit, no longer made sense. He was wealthy and owned a huge corporation. If he loved his daughter so much, would he really kill her fiancé?

"Why didn't you mention this before?"

"Well... um. I suppose I didn't want to accuse anyone of something so serious without knowing the facts. Just because I heard a disagreement doesn't imply someone's guilty of a crime. I owe Preston a lot." Ted twisted his paper napkin in his hands.

I cocked my head to the side. "What do you mean?" I supposed I could have understood not wanting to be the one to point a finger at the boss, but I figured more dirt remained under the surface of his reasoning.

"You see, I developed a terrible gambling addiction. I didn't tell my wife. If she found out, it would devastate her. She'd throw me out of the house and divorce me. I confided in my friend, and he let me pick up some extra hours so I could start paying off some of my debt, and my wife, Rose, wouldn't have to know." By the time he finished, his brow dripped with sweat. He had twisted the napkin he held until it ripped in half.

"Are you hiding anything else?" I asked.

"No. That's everything. You aren't going to tell her, are you?" His eyes begged me for discretion.

I lifted my chin and shot him a disapproving glance down my nose. "It's not my place. You should have brought this up sooner. We'll need the name of your bookie, so I can verify your story."

"He goes by Joe Dawson. I'm sorry I didn't come forward. I am just so ashamed of myself," he replied as his voice cracked. He was a broken man, and I believed him.

I relented. "Thank you. I appreciate you telling me the truth, and I won't tell your wife."

We exchanged our goodbyes, and I walked out to my car. I texted Caleb to ask him if he could conduct a background check on Joe Dawson.

While I waited to hear from him, I ordered some dinner from China Garden. My stomach grumbled. The food would be ready in about fifteen minutes, and the restaurant wasn't far. I chilled in my car to waste time and cranked up the radio while I checked messages on my phone.

After my wait was up, I made my way to the restaurant to pick up my order. Once I arrived home, the girls greeted me by meowing their discontent at my absence. They followed me from the front door to the kitchen.

The Wor Sue Gai smelled amazing. I hated eating with plastic utensils from carryout containers, so I got out a plate and silverware. The girls' voices rose as they expressed their starvation and neglect at my uncaring hands. I sighed and cut up some chicken into tiny bits, which I spooned onto a couple of saucers.

They almost snatched the food from my hands before I had a chance to set it down. Happy feline mumbling filled the air as they voraciously attacked the offering. Maybe it wasn't the healthiest thing, but a treat every so often wouldn't hurt. I finished my portion and placed the leftovers in the fridge.

After I washed the few dishes I'd used, I checked my phone for any messages or missed calls. Caleb still hadn't reached out. I tried his cell again. He picked up on the third ring.

"Hey, sorry I haven't responded to you. Something came up with another of my other cases," he explained.

"It's okay. No worries. Did you research that name I sent you?" I asked.

"Yeah. I talked to a new friend over at the Ashford PD. Turns out, he's a low-level criminal, based out of Columbus. What's the deal with this Dawson, anyway?"

"I met with Ted Banks earlier and found out he has quite the gambling problem. The night of the rehearsal dinner, he left the room to place a call to his bookmaker and overheard an argument."

Caleb's voice perked up. "Who was arguing, and what was it about?"

"He wasn't certain about the subject, but he knew one of the voices belonged to Preston Coleman. Speaking of him, did you talk to Luke?"

"I did. He agrees that we shouldn't act. He's going to set some officers up to monitor the Coleman's home and the Body by Mimi's office."

"How soon could we expect that to happen?"

"I'm not sure. They have protocols to follow. The department's small staff is being stretched thin right now between this case and their other day-to-day stuff."

"Why don't we go do a little surveillance? Then we can share what we find with the police."

"You do realize it's more than sitting in a car, Jordan."

I scoffed. "It can't be that hard."

"What would you do if someone were to approach you?"

"Make up a story and drive off, I guess."

Caleb let out a long sigh. "I have a lot to teach you. How about we go out tomorrow or the following day?"

"Great! I look forward to it," I responded.

"Let's meet up in the morning, and we'll figure out our next plan of action."

"Fine. I'll talk to you tomorrow."

I put away the dishes and put water in the bowls for the girls before making myself a drink to unwind. That was easier said than done. My mind kept thinking if we didn't act soon, we could miss out on the opportunity to solve this case once and for all.

An hour passed, and I continued to mull over the test results we located in the papers in Morgan's office. I walked over to the kitchen table and flipped through the stack of papers and plucked the test results from the pile and turned on my laptop.

I searched and the results brought up a lot of chemical structures and articles regarding beauty, wellness and skincare. As I continued to skim the results, I still couldn't figure out what the reason for those test results could have been. Someone who could help came to mind. My old co-worker Kaci was a chemist at my old lab.

Relieved that I saw her name still in my contacts on my phone, I wasted no time hitting dial.

"Leah, what are you doing calling me this late?" Kaci asked. "Long time no talk."

"Hey, you. I know, I'm sorry. It has been hectic since I came back home, the funeral, settling my aunt's estate, and taking over the family business," I responded.

She let out a low whistle. "Girl, I do not envy you. Are you calling because you want to come back?"

I chuckled. "You wish. No, I think I've closed that chapter for now."

"You can't blame me for missing you. I get it though. What's up?"

"I have some lab results, and I wondered if you could take a look at them and let me know if you notice anything off?"

"Sure. Do you want to email them to me? I'm in between a couple tests right now, so I can take a gander."

"Great. Let me screenshot them, and I will send them over. Let me know when you receive it."

"While we wait, any new guys in your life?" she asked.

I groaned. "Yes, no, maybe."

Kaci laughed. "That's a yes. I want to hear everything about him! Is he cute? Does he have a good job? When do I get to meet him?"

"Whoa, whoa, tap the brakes! I am not even sure what's going on with either one of them."

She gasped. "Did you say two? Leah, you bad girl!"

I really didn't want to get into it right now. "That's a story for another time. Did you receive my email?"

"Let me check. Yep, got it. Gimme a couple of minutes to look it over."

I waited with growing impatience while she scanned the documents.

"Hmm, this is weird," she murmured.

I pounced on the comment. "What's that?" I asked.

"It appears the sample tested was a body wash. Checking over the ingredients, it seems, pretty standard, but the quantities look odd."

"Odd how?"

"In any product, you have to use a certain amount of each ingredient to create the formula. In this case, however, the amount of water to what would typically be in a normal body wash is twice as much as it should be," she explained.

"Son of a gun! You have got to be kidding me! They're watering it down that much?" I gasped. "The manufacturers are cheating their customers!"

"Sadly, yes. It's not uncommon, but it's also not something you see all the time. Does that help at all? Or do you still have more questions?" she asked.

"No. That helps a lot," I replied.

"What does this have to do with wedding planning?"

"It's a long story. We'll have to meet for lunch sometime, and I will explain. For now, I need to go. Thank you so much for all your help!"

"You're welcome. I will hold you to it. I would love to see you."

"After we hung up, I dialed Caleb's number, He was not going to believe this. Morgan must have found out what his future father-in-law was doing and threatened to blow the whistle. The phone rang, but he did not pick up. I tried a couple more times and decided just to leave a voicemail.

"Ugh! This couldn't wait any longer. I picked up my purse and went out the door.

CHAPTER EIGHTEEN

Surveillance wasn't exciting. I'd been waiting across from the Coleman home for hours now. No movement. Not a peep...zilch! I reclined in my seat and stretched. Who knew sitting in a vehicle would be so exhausting?

Just as I closed my eyes, I could hear a motor approaching in the distance. I picked the newspaper up from the front passenger side next to me and slid down further. It passed, and I peered out. Bingo!

The dark-colored sedan matched the one Devin witnessed at The Wedded Bliss. I started my engine and pulled out onto the road. On all the crime shows I'd watched, the person following always kept a safe distance from their target.

It headed out of the Riverton Estates neighborhood, turning left on Copper Road. Traffic wasn't too heavy, thankfully, and I could keep the car in view. It continued west out of town. The vehicle turned into the Ashford Industrial Park. I stayed back and waited a few seconds before entering myself. I passed the first driveway and veered down the second one.

I switched off my headlights and parked in the shadows. Reaching over to the passenger seat, I picked up my flashlight, phone, and pepper spray. I slipped out of the car and made my way to the Body by Mimi building.

My luck at getting to it unseen caused me to breathe a sigh of relief before I crept around the side. I saw the sedan positioned close to the front.

I sneaked up to the double entrance doors and tried the left initially, but it didn't budge. Holding my breath and crossing my fingers, I tested the right one next, and it opened on the first try. I stepped in and kept hold of the handle in order to ease it shut as quietly as possible. Once inside, I first noticed a small passage straight ahead that stopped at another corridor, allowing me to go either direction once I hit the end.

I chose the hallway to my left. About halfway down, I could see illumination coming from under one of the doors. I silently passed what I assumed to be various offices and labs before I reached it. I bent forward to peek through the small rectangular window.

A male of average height stood at a lab counter with his back to me. I moved closer for a better view to see if I could discover his identity. Keeping my body off to the left of the glass pane, I leaned over to the side. I went a bit too far because the next thing I knew, I lost my balance and fell to the right. My hand shot out to catch myself on the doorframe as my knee hit the door. The loud noise startled him inside, and he spun around.

Crap!

I ducked and scurried down the hall. I found another doorway to slip into and still be able to keep an eye out in case the guy came my way. A few seconds later, Preston Coleman stuck his head out, looking both ways. I gasped and covered my mouth, hoping he hadn't heard me.

My heart pounded, and a few minutes later, my breathing slowed. After what felt like an eternity, he left the lab and headed down the hallway away from me. I continued to creep down the corridor in the opposite direction to the end. A glowing exit sign caught my eye further down. If I could just make it there and go back to my car, I could call Caleb and tell him what I found out.

Peering out into the passage and seeing no sign of Janie's dad or anyone else, I proceeded with all manner of caution toward the red sign to freedom. I reached out to grab the knob. Just before my fingers touched it, a heavy hand latched onto my left shoulder. It yanked me back and forced me down the hallway.

"Ow! You're hurting me!!" I exclaimed. I tried to squirm free, but I couldn't dislodge his iron grip, which kept me facing forward.

"Good! You just couldn't let it go, could you? Morgan's dead, and no one would miss him," Preston grumbled.

"You killed him. Why? Why would you do that to Janie?" I turned my head back to look at him.

"He was a low-class loser. Do you think my beautiful, well-off, intelligent daughter deserved a blackmailing piece of trash for a husband? No! She deserves the best!" The more he talked, the louder he became. The veins in his neck bulged, and his face grew red.

I could agree with most of his statements, but intelligent? "Why didn't you stop it before it came to this?" I asked.

"I had no clue at first who the little jerk was until he started blackmailing me. He looked familiar, but I couldn't put my finger on it. Until I saw one of the old pictures hanging in the executive hallway. Then all the pieces fell into place," Preston groused.

"Can you blame him for wanting to expose you? You were cheating customers!" I exclaimed. "What even possessed you to water down your products?"

"The recession killed the economy, and costs became way too high for ingredients. It would ruin me. I couldn't let that happen," he grumbled. "All the blood, sweat, tears, and hard work I sank into the company. No one—and I mean no one—would take it from me. I'm Preston Ellsworth Coleman!"

Wow. He was even more full of himself than I thought. As we reached another crossroads in the hallway, I attempted to twist free and get away. I didn't manage it. He expected me to try something and slammed me into the wall. Tears stung my eyes as a sharp pain lanced through my left shoulder. I would not let him see me cry, so I bit my lower lip to keep from screaming out. I tried to move it, but it hurt so much, he may have broken it.

He pulled out a pocketknife and held it at my back, forcing me to continue down the hall.

"Don't even think about it. No one else knows the truth, so once I dispose of you, the murder investigation will go stagnant, and everyone will overlook poor little Morgan...or should I say, Jason."

The longer Coleman talked, the crazier and more unstable he sounded. How could this be the same professional and intimidating man I met before? My mind raced, trying to figure out my options. I already tried to make a break for it, and that was an epic failure. If I kept him talking, maybe I could distract him long enough to reach my phone.

I hated to admit it, but Caleb was right. I shouldn't have jumped the gun on surveillance without someone else. Too late now. He would not let me live this down. That is, if I made it out of here.

We proceeded down the hall, and Preston stopped in front of a solid cream door with a keypad. He punched in a code, and it unlocked. He shoved me through the doorway first, keeping a tight grasp on my injured shoulder. The room appeared to be another lab of some sort, very plain and sterile with white walls.

Tall, black metal cabinets lined the far wall across from the entrance. In the middle were two large counters placed four to five feet apart, each with a sink, drawers, and cupboards. Standing near them were a pair of plastic and aluminum chairs. The only windows were rectangular in shape and high up on the wall.

Preston pulled a chair over to the nearest counter and forced me into it. He opened a drawer where he found a packet of zip ties. Keeping his hold on me, he shook the contents onto the work surface. Only one remained inside. Grumbling, he took it out and secured my left wrist to the sturdy cupboard handle under the drawer.

I might have been able to free myself, but the blinding agony in my shoulder made me so dizzy it took everything I had to remain conscious. A tear slid down my face. I didn't want to die like this, at the hands of a crooked businessman doing all he could to keep from getting caught.

Coleman walked over to the first cabinet and rooted around, with his back to me. While his attention was diverted, I reached into my right pocket with my free hand and retrieved my cell phone. I scrolled through my call history and dialed Caleb. I turned the volume all the way down in case his voice was audible, placed my phone back in, and made sure the speaker faced out. Someone had to know what was happening, especially if I didn't make it out of here.

Labs used all sorts of equipment. Maybe I could find a pair of scissors to free myself. I rose to my feet and slid open the well-oiled drawer where my captor found the ties. Taking great care to be quiet, I scooted some things around inside. Bingo! A plastic-sheathed razor knife would do the trick. I took the cover off with my teeth and put the blade to the restraint. Just as I started to cut, Mr. Coleman closed the cabinet and strode over to me.

"I thought I told you not to move," he barked and snatched at the instrument I held. "Thought you could get away, eh?"

His aim was off and instead of grabbing it, he knocked it out of my hand. It skidded across the counter and rattled into the sink where it promptly went down the drain.

"Sorry, I had to stretch my legs," I replied. "You don't have to do this."

It was now or never. I yanked on my wrist and the plastic snapped. The action caused a sharp stab of pain in my injured shoulder that almost knocked me to my knees. Before I could run, he clamped down on my other arm and shoved me back down into the chair.

"Of course, I do. Now that you're aware of everything." Preston had some type of tubing in his hand. He unwound it. Next, he grasped my arms and forced them behind the seat.

The sudden movement was agonizing, and I let out a small gasp.

"I tried to warn you. Why didn't you take the hints? No, you just had to keep snooping."

"Hints?" My brain had trouble focusing on Coleman's words since it was a little preoccupied with his plans for my demise. After a couple of minutes, it clicked. "That was you the night at Morgan's condominium, wasn't it? And you were the one who sent me the dead bird ..."

"You and that friend of yours surprised me. I didn't expect anyone to be there," he replied.

"And the bird? The damage to The Wedded Bliss?"

"The feathered gift was a subtle tactic to dissuade you from investigating. Apparently, it didn't work the way I had hoped."

"How could you do that to my business? As one owner to another, that's so awful!"

"I became desperate. You were getting too close to the truth," he grumbled.

"You think you'll just get away with everything? People will be looking for me!"

"Not when they find a note written by you telling them you left town. And your car will end up at the bottom of the Hoover Reservoir," He finished tying my hands and bent down to tie my legs.

I tried to kick him, but he clamped a big hand around my ankle and crushed it against the chair leg as he secured me to it. Not caring to be quiet anymore, I let out a shriek. "No one is going to believe you!" I moved my arms to see if I could loosen them.

"Just you wait. Money talks. You'd be surprised what a small amount of green can do. You should know firsthand. Not only will you disappear, but your precious little business also becomes obsolete."

"Is this necessary?" I asked, wriggling hard.

"Stop moving! You're not going anywhere."

Coleman left the room, and I took my chance. I started rocking the chair back and forth but my efforts had no effect.

"Caleb, if you still hear me, please get here. I'm at the Body by Mimi's office building in one of the labs. I can't tell you where, but I see what looks like parking lights shining in the top windows. Bring backup. Call Luke and..."

Before I could finish, Coleman stormed into the room.

"Who are you talking to? And why is the chair moved? I thought I told you to be still!" he yelled.

I shook my head. "No one!"

"I don't believe you," he sneered.

He strode over and patted me down. I hoped my phone would just blend in and he wouldn't notice it.

As his hand reached closer to my pocket, I tried to distract him. "Are those headlights reflecting off the ceiling? The police must be on their way!"

Lot of good that did. He found the phone and snatched it from me.

"Son-of-a...who did you call? Doesn't matter." My captor tossed it onto the floor and stomped on it. "You idiot!"

He paced around, muttering to himself. With his attention elsewhere, I seized the opportunity to rock the chair again, desperately trying to loosen something. It fell over. The noise caught his attention. He rushed over and slammed my head down on the ground.

He used such force everything went black.

"Leah? Talk to me. Are you okay?"

"Can you open your eyes?"

Two different voices spoke to me. The pounding and throbbing in my skull made it impossible to concentrate on anything. That plus the ringing in my ears caused me to feel as though I had gone ten rounds in a boxing ring. My swollen shoulder was on fire. I moaned, and when I cracked open my left eye, I realized the investigator and the cop were staring down at me with concern plastered all over their faces.

"Are you going to be okay if we pick you up now?" Caleb asked.

My fingers and toes were numb and tingling. "I can't feel my hands or feet," I replied.

"We'll be gentle," Luke promised. "We just have to untie you to get your circulation flowing."

"Plus, the EMTs will have to examine you," Caleb added. "On three. One. Two. Three."

They both gripped an end of the chair and gently set me right side up. The movement made me woozy, and a wave of nausea hit me.

"Let's get her free," Luke murmured.

Caleb untied my hands while Luke freed my feet and placed the tubing in a paper evidence bag. I noticed they both wore white latex gloves so they wouldn't contaminate any evidence.

"Bring the gurney in now, please," Caleb called out.

A team of EMTs entered the room, two men and a woman. They carefully positioned me on the stretcher, and the female checked my vitals.

"Coleman. Where is he?" I rasped.

The investigator peered over the EMT's shoulder. "Once he heard the sirens approaching, he ran. Strickland sent cruisers to follow him."

Luke chimed in. "After a short while, an officer stopped him on the other end of town before he could reach the freeway."

"Don't worry about that right now. We can talk more about it later. Let's just get you to the hospital," Caleb advised.

The EMTs finished their initial assessment, covered me with a sheet, strapped me down, and took me out to the ambulance.

I heard Luke say, "Hamilton, you go with her. Let's meet up in a bit. I need to finish up here first."

"Sounds good," Caleb replied as he leaned over to shake the other man's hand. "I'll take great care of her."

The entire ride was surreal. You watched them on television, but being the patient in the back of an ambulance is weird. The bumps were few and far between, but when we hit one, tortuous pain flushed through my entire body.

"Leah, I need you to wiggle your fingers for me," the female EMT directed.

I tried to obey as much as I could. The tingling felt awful.

"Now your toes?" she asked, taking notes on her little notepad.

I did my best, but they didn't feel like they moved.

"Okay good," she replied, writing again.

"Am I going to be okay?" I questioned, making direct eye contact, striving to understand my current condition.

"You're stable, but we won't know the extent of your injuries till they run some tests. They will get your head wound cleaned and send you for a CT scan. That way, they can make sure there isn't more serious damage," she explained.

A few hours later, after blood work, an MRI, and more poking and prodding, Dr. Rodriquez determined I only had a mild concussion and was a very lucky woman. The circulation returned to normal, and the tingling had diminished in my hands and feet. The doctor still wanted to keep me overnight for observation and to monitor me.

Caleb stuck it out with me the entire time, and Luke stopped over later. My best friends both dropped by to check on me. Chelsea offered to head to my house to feed and look in on the cats, while Meg told me not to worry about things at The Wedded Bliss. She and Sally would have it all under control.

They were the best. It took some stress off me knowing I left everything in excellent hands. The pain meds they gave me were nice but made me sleepy. The girls left first. Caleb and Luke stayed around a little longer, but I couldn't keep my eyes open. The guys both agreed to leave me to rest.

The next day, I woke up feeling like a semi had hit me. The nurse entered and handed me my meds, and my food tray was delivered. Thank God! I was starving. I removed the lid and the delicious aroma of breakfast wafted into my face. They'd given me pancakes, sausage links, and some scrambled eggs. It all looked delicious.

Caleb strolled in with a beautiful bouquet of brightly colored flowers. Followed by Luke carrying an adorable brown teddy bear.

"Morning. I didn't expect to see you so early." I set my silverware to the side.

They placed their offerings on the wide windowsill and settled down around me. Caleb took the seat on the right of my bed while Meg's brother pulled a chair over and sat to my left.

"I can't stay too long. Still have to lots to do," Luke muttered.

That was understandable. I couldn't imagine all the paperwork and ends to tie up that had to go with solving a case. The way he spoke made me think he would have rather kept me company instead, which sent a warm tingle through my heart.

Caleb unzipped his jacket and crossed his legs. "We wanted to see how you were doing and talk to you about last night."

"So, how did you locate me?" I asked.

"Your idea to call me on your cellphone was genius. I tracked your phone and found your GPS location," he answered.

"When the signal went dead, Hamilton alerted me, and we dispatched all available cruisers to the Body by Mimi building," Luke explained, pulling out his note pad.

I looked over at Caleb and sighed. "Go ahead. Tell me I should have listened to you. You were right." As much as it pained me to do so, I admitted it.

"I think you know what you did was dangerous. I won't rub it in. I'm just glad you're okay." Caleb reached over and squeezed my hand. He left it there for a few moments.

Luke cleared his throat. "Why don't you start at the beginning and tell us what transpired?"

Caleb released his grip and readjusted in his chair.

It would be best to get it over with, so I dove right in. "I thought I'd do some surveillance. I figured if anything happened, I would call Caleb. However, the car Devin witnessed left the Coleman residence, and I followed. My adrenaline probably fueled my decision, but I knew I had to see where it was going."

Both sighed in unison.

"Do you want to let me continue before you two grumble at me?" I asked, glancing back and forth between them.

Luke gestured with his hand. "Go ahead."

"Sorry," Caleb mumbled.

At least the investigator appeared contrite instead of irritated like the cop did.

"The building's parking lot was empty except for the car I tailed. I turned into the next driveway and found a spot behind some trees before I got out and approached the building. I discovered an unlocked door and kept snooping.

"How did you know you were following Preston Coleman?" Luke asked.

"To be completely honest, I didn't at first. Once I got inside, I discovered the building was a maze of hallways. After creeping around for a minute, I noticed a room with its lights on, so I peeked in the little window. That's when I saw him."

"Why not leave then and call one of us?" Caleb interrupted.

"I tried! I almost reached the exit door when he caught me. I struggled to get away, but he had me by the shoulder in a painful grip I couldn't break and slammed me into the wall." My hand unconsciously went to the injury.

"That son of a—" Luke bit back the rest of his curse and took a second to compose himself. "Go on."

"The jerk dragged me back down the hall to the lab where you found me. At first, he forced me to sit in a chair and zip-tied one of my wrists to the cupboard handle. He didn't think to search me for a phone right away, so while he looked for something better to tie me up with, I managed to dial my cell to reach out to you before he restrained me." I shuddered at the awful memory.

"What happened after that?" Luke asked.

"While his back was turned, I found a razor knife in the drawer beside me, but as I cut the plastic around my wrist, he came back and caught me. He grabbed for the knife but hit it instead, and it fell into the sink and down the drain. He shoved me back into the chair and tied me to it with the rubber tubing you saw. Coleman admitted he killed Morgan and knocked me down the other night at his residence. The dead bird, the vandalism, all him."

"I'm glad he didn't get the blade!" Caleb gasped. "If he got hold of it, he could have stabbed you or cut you with it!"

"You were in the victim's condo? It was a potential crime scene!" the cop exclaimed at the same time.

"Long story. Apparently, his future son-in-law found out about them watering down the Body by Mimi products and threatened to go to the Better Business Bureau and the media outlets exposing him."

"That's a good motive," Caleb commented.

"Blackmailing him did Morgan no favors. It only served to piss Coleman off" I explained.

"Keep going. What happened next?" Luke prompted.

"I tried everything I could think of to prolong the conversation. I hoped to stall long enough for someone to get there. Then he ordered me to be still. At one point, he left the room and that's when I tried to move to undo the restraints."

"Did he lay his hands on you? I mean did he hit you or choke you?" Caleb demanded.

"No, everything he did was minor. I was rocking the chair back and forth and lost my balance. The next thing I knew, you two were standing over me." I'd momentarily forgotten Preston had been the one to smack my head into the floor, knocking me out.

"You are very lucky, Leah. He could have killed you!" Caleb exclaimed.

I held my hand up to the side of my head. His concern touched me, but did he have to be so loud? "He didn't though. What happens now?"

"Coleman will face arraignment, and the court has to schedule a bail hearing," Luke explained. "The prosecuting attorney will ask for pretrial release to be revoked.

"You don't have to stress yourself about that. He'll go away for a long time." Caleb added.

"Your friend is right. You just need to get better."

"Do you guys have any more questions? I should finish my food, and I'm getting sleepy," I yawned.

Luke stood and reached out to shake my hand. "I think we're good. Thank you again for letting us come by. I know this hasn't been easy. You'll need to stop by the station in the next day or two and sign your official statement, but for today I've got what I need."

So formal.

"If you need a ride later, call me. I'd be glad to pick you up," Caleb offered.

I told Hamilton, I would let him know, and they both left. I only ate about half my breakfast and passed out.

They released me later that day, and I returned to The Wedded Bliss a couple of days later. The Coleman family called a television press conference, and we all planned to meet and gather around the TV to watch. Janie's mother resembled a dog with her tail between her legs. Preston's actions shamed the family, and she issued a full apology to The Wedded Bliss, the community, and their valued customers. She ended by advising that the company would take this time to regroup and reorganize and would make a formal statement at a later date.

Once the conference ended, Sally turned off the television. We all sat in silence.

Meg spoke first. "Wow, that must have been pretty difficult for her."

"You don't think she knew anything about any of it?" Chelsea asked.

"No. She may have been the face of Body by Mimi, but Preston ran everything," Sally chimed in.

I sighed. "I'm just glad it's over."

"Me too," Chelsea agreed.

"Let's celebrate!" I exclaimed.

Chelsea held up her hands. "Wait, there's something else. Mrs. Coleman issued a check for the full amount they owed for the wedding, plus more. Probably out of guilt, but you know what that means, right?"

"What?" The rest of us looked at her.

"I've gone over the books and crunched the numbers. The Wedded Bliss is staying open!" she cheered.

"Are you serious?" I asked.

"Yep. Between the work Meg and I accomplished on getting accounts caught up and the payment from Mrs. Coleman, we'll be able to catch up on the mortgage and have a little left over," she explained.

"That is wonderful!" Happy tears filled my eyes. "You guys are the best team, no make that family."

"We do work pretty well, together, don't we?" Meg chuckled with a wink.

"Your Aunt Sissy would be so proud of you, Leah. She is smiling down on us right now," Sally beamed.

"Thank you. That means a lot. We have big things ahead, hosting our first show and gracing the cover of the Buckeye Brides Wedding Guide. I wouldn't want to do it with anyone else."

Sally left the room briefly and came back in with a small cheesecake, plates, and forks. Meg poured everyone a fresh cup of coffee while we enjoyed the treat.

"To The Wedded Bliss!" we cheered.

WEDDING TIPS

Budgeting

An important step in the wedding planning process is to determine how much you have to spend on your event. Per The Knot 2022 Real Wedding Study, the average cost of a wedding is $30,000.

Traditionally, a bride's parents or family pay for the wedding. It will be important to have discussed with them about whether they plan to provide money for the wedding and how much they can contribute. Times have changed, as well as family dynamics. Some couples even choose to pay for their own weddings.

Budgets can be as simple or as detailed as you need, whether it's big or small. It can also vary from couple to couple. You can make notes, put together a spreadsheet, or, if you are more of a visual learner, create a diagram with pictures or even a color-coded chart. You can also adjust the amounts or percentages allotted higher or lower for the different areas depending on your preferences or needs. The largest percentage of your budget will be the venue at 35-50%. The second highest allotment will be for catering or food. If you select a venue that includes catering or food, then you can make adjustments accordingly. Afterward, you will allocate the rest of your budget to the remaining categories.

The categories you want to include on your list are (but not limited to):

- Venue

- Catering

- Cake

- Wedding Attire

- Entertainment

- Flowers

- Rentals

- Photography

- Videography

- Rentals

- Wedding planner

- Invitations

- Transportation

- Hair and Makeup

- Officiant

- Favors and Gifts

- Decor

Once you establish your budget, you can start researching and making your choices for each of the categories. You also want to allow room for additional fees or costs you may encounter along the way. Track your spending as you select and reserving vendors. Then you can adjust your budget as needed.

Things to remember when budgeting for your wedding:

1. Set realistic expectations about what you can afford.

2. Decide from the beginning what are the priorities for your special day.

3. Determine a guest list size that will fit within your budget and be firm.

4. Venues can vary depending on their location, fees, and headcount requirements.

5. Weddings during the height of wedding season between May and October will have higher costs.

6. Style also plays a role. A fancier wedding will be more expensive than a simpler wedding.

7. Plan to include overages in your budget for each area as a safety net.

8. Don't let fear hold you back from bargain shopping, taking advantage of sales, and doing a little DIY to save money.

9. Consider investing in special event insurance.

Wedding Planners

What do wedding planners do?

Wedding planners assist couples with the planning process and steps leading up to their special day and on the day of the event.

Why should you use a wedding planner?

They can help ease stress and use their knowledge, skills, and experience to help create you and your significant other the best day it can be.

How do you find a wedding planner?

First, you need to decide what type of services you require. Do you need someone to assist with all the different aspects of planning or do you need someone to help with certain sections like assisting on the day of, or working with vendors, etc? Once you have decided what type you need, then you can research them. Using local resources, attending bridal shows, or getting recommendations from people you know.

What types of wedding planners are there?

There are several types of wedding planners depending on your requirements or needs.

- Full-service or all-inclusive: They will assist you with planning from A to Z, selecting vendors, and deciding during the process. Great for busy couples who don't have time or need help with decisions.

- Month of planner: They work with you in the last few weeks or days leading up to your special day. Focusing on finalizing contracts, deliveries, and details and dealing with last-minute issues.

- Weekend wedding coordinator: They will not only assist on the wedding day but can help with handling guests, and planning and coordinating wedding-related events such as rehearsal dinners.

- Day of coordinator: They help make sure your special day goes well with minor issues. Such as making sure vendors arrive on time, directing them where to go, and handling all the minor details so the couple can focus on their special day.

- Destination wedding coordinator: If you choose to have a destination wedding, they can help with local venues, vendors, and information for your special day.

- Scouting venues and giving referrals: These planners will recommend and show you venue options, help negotiate contracts, and connect you with vendors they are familiar with.

- À la carte: If you do not require a full-service or all-inclusive plan, you can work with these individuals and hire them for certain services you may need.

How much do wedding planners cost?

The cost for a wedding planner can vary depending on what services you need to hire them for. The full-service or all-inclusive planners will be more expensive than just hiring one as a day-of coordinator. Depending on where you live can also factor into how much they may charge for their services.

ACKNOWLEDGEMENTS

To my number one supporter from day one, my mom–Thank you for always encouraging me to pursue my dreams. I am so thankful you got to witness me finishing my first manuscript before you passed. I did it Mom! 143 forever and always.

To my Dad–Thank you for believing in me.

To my husband and kids–Your unwavering support means the world. Thank you for being my biggest cheerleaders!

To my best friend Julia–You have been through thick and thin with me over the last twenty-plus years and there are not enough words to tell you how much I appreciate you, our friendship, and your support on this publishing journey.

To the CCC group Ann, and Kris–Thank you for being wonderful accountability members, critique partners, and friends.

To my Beta readers Mary, Barb, Marise, and Lora–Thank you for taking the time to read my book and give me feedback. I appreciate it more than you know.

To my family and friends–Thank you for supporting me, asking about my writing, and listening to me talk about my writing.

Photo credit: Christian Temelkoski | chrisTphotos

Small Towns. Quirky Characters. Hidden Secrets.

Christine Lawrence resides in a small town in Northwest Ohio with her husband, stepdaughter, son, and four spoiled dogs. An avid reader since childhood, she decided to mesh her two favorite genres, romance and mystery. Working hard to complete the next book in The Wedded Bliss mystery series, she spends her free time participating in local writing groups, traveling, and spending time with her family.

Christine has a bachelor's degree in forensic science with a specialization in Crime Scene Investigation and a master's degree in forensic psychology. Her background as a private investigator and obsession with all things crime related gives her endless fodder for her small-town cozy mysteries.

9 798991 088503